Everything reminded him of Aimee.

Hunter caught his breath as her image flooded his mind. Aimee, with her big dark eyes and sexy contralto voice. Aimee, always laughing, bringing him out of himself and into the world of the living. Aimee, in his arms, his bed, his life.

He curled his fingers into his palms, the memory of her so sharp he winced. Since his plane had touched down at New Orleans International, he'd been unable to stop thinking of her. She was from a Cajun fishing village not far from here. He'd found himself looking for her, listening for her.

Hunter frowned. It had been years since she'd walked out of his life. Or rather, since he'd driven her out of it. He'd thought of her. He'd missed her. But he'd never considered going after her. He'd had nothing to give her.

His frown deepened.

He still didn't.

Dear Reader,

Welcome to Silhouette **Special Edition** . . . welcome to romance.

Last year, I requested that you send me your opinions on the books that we publish, and on romances in general. Thank you so much for the many thoughtful letters. For the next couple of months, I'd like to share some quotes from these letters with you. This seemed very appropriate now while we are in the midst of the THAT SPECIAL WOMAN! promotion. Each one of our readers is a special woman, as heroic as the heroines in our books.

This September has some wonderful stories coming your way. *A Husband to Remember* by Lisa Jackson is our THAT SPECIAL WOMAN! selection for this month.

This month also has other special treats. For one, we've got *Bride Wanted* by Debbie Macomber coming your way. This is the second book in her FROM THIS DAY FORWARD series. *Night Jasmine* by Erica Spindler—one of the BLOSSOMS OF THE SOUTH series—is also on its way to happy readers, as is Laurie Paige's *A Place for Eagles,* the second tale in her WILD RIVER TRILOGY. And September brings more books from favorite authors Patricia Coughlin and Natalie Bishop.

I hope you enjoy this book, and all of the stories to come!

Sincerely,

Tara Gavin
Senior Editor
Silhouette Books

Quote of the Month: "All the Silhouettes I've read have believable characters and are easy to identify with. The pace of the story line is good, the books hold my interest. When I start a Silhouette, I know I'm in for a good time."
—P. Digney,
New Jersey

ERICA
SPINDLER

NIGHT JASMINE

Silhouette®

SPECIAL EDITION®

Published by Silhouette Books New York

America's Publisher of Contemporary Romance

For Karen (Young) Stone,
quintessential Southern flower,
friend and confidante,
roomie and phone junkie

Thanks for sharing your Southernness with me!
(And Thibodaux, too!)

SILHOUETTE BOOKS
300 East 42nd St., New York, N.Y. 10017

NIGHT JASMINE

Copyright © 1993 by Erica Spindler

ISBN: 0-373-09838-3

First Silhouette Books printing September 1993

Printed in the U.S.A.

Books by Erica Spindler

Silhouette Special Edition

Longer Than... #696
Baby Mine #728
*A Winter's Rose #817
*Night Jasmine #838

Silhouette Desire

Heaven Sent #442
Chances Are #482
Read Between the Lines #538

*Blossoms of the South

ERICA SPINDLER

believes in love at first date. Because that's all the time it took for her and her husband, Nathan, to fall in love. "We were too young. We both had to finish college. Our parents thought we should see other people, but we knew we were meant for each other," Erica says. Thirteen years later, they still know it.

Erica chose her home—Louisiana—the same way. She went "way down yonder" for a visit, fell in love with the state and decided to stay. "I may have been born in the Midwest," she says, "but I'm a true Southerner at heart." It is that continuing love affair with the people and customs of the South that inspired Erica to write her Blossoms of the South trilogy.

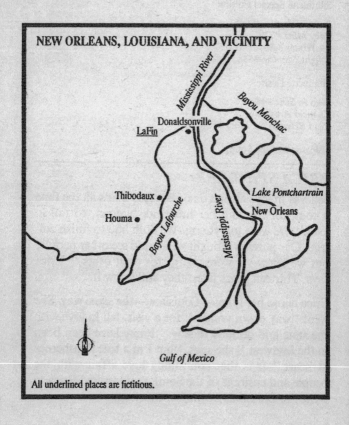

NEW ORLEANS, LOUISIANA, AND VICINITY

Mississippi River

Bayou Manchac

Donaldsonville

LaFin

Thibodaux

Houma

Bayou Lafourche

Mississippi River

Lake Pontchartrain

New Orleans

N

Gulf of Mexico

All underlined places are fictitious.

Prologue

April sun spilled over Hunter Powell, warming him. That same light reflected off the New Orleans pavement, blinding and white, and he cursed himself for having left his sunglasses back at the convention center.

Hunter stuck with his fellow doctors as they made their way through the throngs of tourists crowding the French Quarter sidewalks, unsure of how—or why—he had gotten himself hooked up with them. Drinking mind-numbing concoctions and tramping in and out of T-shirt shops was not his idea of a good time.

And yet, here he was.

The group made its way onto the more refined and less trafficked Royal Street. The sounds here were mellower—taps striking the pavement as a panhandler danced for quarters, the whisper of the breeze, thick with the scent of boiling seafood, occasional bursts of laughter, rich with amusement.

Everything reminded him of Aimee.

Hunter caught his breath as her image flooded his mind. Aimee—with her big dark eyes and sexy contralto voice. Aimee, always laughing, bringing him out of himself and into the world of the living. Aimee in his arms, his bed, his life.

Hunter curled his fingers into his palms, the memory of her so sharp he winced. Since his plane had touched down at New Orleans International Airport two days before, he'd been unable to stop thinking of her. He'd found himself looking for her, listening for her.

He shook his head. Only because she was from a Cajun fishing village not far from here, he reasoned. Only because she'd laughed so often about its name— La Fin, "the end" in French.

Hunter drew his eyebrows together. It had been three and a half years since she'd walked out of his life. Or rather, he amended, since he'd driven her out of it. And in all that time he'd never questioned that her leaving had been for the best. Oh, he'd thought of her. He'd missed her. But he'd never considered going after her.

He'd had nothing to give her. He still didn't.

Hunter's frown deepened. The reminiscing stopped now, he decided. It was a foolish waste of time and energy; it bordered on maudlin. He would go back to the hotel and look over the paper he was scheduled to present in the morning. Just as he'd put Aimee from his life three and a half years ago, he would put her from his mind now.

Hunter dragged his attention from the past to his fellow medical conventioneers, a couple of them already half drunk on a local favorite called a "hurricane." "I'll see you all at dinner. I'm heading back to the hotel."

"Awe, c'mon, Hunter," said Jack, an orthopedic man from Des Moines and one of the ones who was half in the bag, "all work and no play will make you a very dull boy."

"Yeah, Hunter," piped up another colleague whose name Hunter couldn't recall, "you're going to give us doctors a bad name."

"Leave him be, all of you," piped in Sheila, one of the internists from his own clinic in California. "Hunter's got the right idea. My feet are killing me." She turned to Hunter. "I want to take a peek in this shop, then I'll walk back with you."

Hunter lifted his gaze to the shop in question. Small Miracles, the sign proclaimed. Antiques and bric-a-brac. Nodding, he followed Sheila inside.

The interior of the shop was cool and smelled of mildew and mothballs. Intent on waiting until Sheila had seen her fill, Hunter leaned against the counter. As he did, his elbow knocked against an item sitting on the counter's edge. Turning quickly, he caught it a moment before it toppled to the floor.

The object, a domed music box, landed neatly in his hands. Hunter stared at it, his heart beginning to thump against the wall of his chest. Antiques didn't interest him. He'd furnished his own home in clean, modern lines. Simple. No froufrou.

The box in his hands, with its gold filigree and porcelain figurine, was definitely froufrou. He told himself he should set the box back on the counter and be more careful where he put his elbows. Instead he held it up for a closer look.

The figurine, a replica of a southern belle complete with hoop skirt and picture hat, was exquisite. She wore a coquettish expression, and in her hands she held a cluster of white star-shaped blossoms. Hunter wound the box's key and as a romantic Brahms melody filled the air, the figure circled the base, hands out as if offering the flowers.

Hunter stared at the figurine, his mind again flooded with thoughts of Aimee, thoughts so vivid, so sensory, he could almost hear her coaxing laugh, almost feel the brush of her mouth on his flesh. He tightened his fingers on the box's lustrous wood base. Aimee had smelled of sunshine and exotic flowers. She'd tasted as sweet as—

"Night Jasmine," a woman said from behind him, her voice husky and amused.

Startled, Hunter swung around, thinking for one moment that it was Aimee behind him, rather than the tiny woman with flame red hair and a mischievous grin whom he found instead. Night Jasmine. Hunter stared dumbly at the shopkeeper, his mind still on Aimee. Aimee had talked of the night jasmine that grew wild near her home, had spoken of the warm spring evenings in the bayou when its scent would become almost overpoweringly potent.

"Excuse me?" he managed after a moment, knowing he must appear an idiot.

"The flowers," the shopkeeper said, motioning to the figurine. "They're night jasmine. Ever heard of them?"

"Yes. Someone I once knew..." Hunter let the thought trail off, turning his gaze back to the music box. "It's a beautiful piece. But I'm not interested in antiques."

"No?" With a deep laugh, the woman took the box from his hands and wound it again. "But this is no ordinary antique. This one is quite special. It's from Ashland, one of the Mississippi delta's best known plantations. Ever heard of it?"

Hunter shook his head. "No, I'm from California, and I really don't care fo—"

"Such a sad tale. The plantation survived the war, but not the times. Anyway, this piece was fashioned for Annabelle Carter upon her betrothal to the master of Ashland, Beauregard Ames." The shopkeeper patted her cap of red curls, and her silver bracelets jangled. "The family hated to let the box go... but you know how it is. These things happen."

Sheila tapped his arm. "Ready, Hunter?"

He looked blankly at her. "Yes... no. In a minute. I'll be out... in a minute." Calling himself fourteen kinds of fool, he turned back to the saleswoman. He didn't need this thing. He didn't even want it. Not really. And yet, he had the strangest reluctance to let it out of his sight. "How much is it?"

"How can we put a price on history?" The little woman sighed dramatically. "But of course we must. It's a steal at eight hundred."

"Eight hundred?" Hunter repeated, good sense making a belated appearance. He shook his head. "Thank you for your time, but I don't think—"

"You will regret forever if you pass it up." She looked him directly in the eye. "It is *very* special."

Hunter blinked, thinking of regrets. And of Aimee and her little fishing village. Not for the first time since arriving in New Orleans he wondered how far from the city that fishing village was, wondered if Aimee would be there.

"You have questions, *cher?*"

Cher. Aimee used to call him that. Only Aimee. Hunter drew his eyebrows together and met the shopkeeper's gaze. "Have you ever heard of a place called La Fin?"

"But, of course." The tiny woman stroked the music box's base as she spoke, a smile curving her lips. "It's about an hour from here. And such a pretty drive. I will give you directions."

Hunter looked back at the box, his chest tight. He acknowledged that the thoughts running through his head were not only totally out of character, but bordered on irrational. Go see Aimee? After all this time? If she were even in La Fin, she would no doubt toss him out on his ear.

"Sometimes, *cher,* we have to follow our gut." The woman cocked her head, her gaze still on his. "Don't you think so?"

Hunter frowned at the shopkeeper, unsettled by the feeling that she was able to read his mind, wishing he could dispute her words. But the hell of it was, he did think so. "I'll give you seven fifty for it."

The little woman smiled, her eyes alight with satisfaction. "You are a hard man, *cher*. But you have a deal."

Chapter One

"This little piggy went to the French Market," Aimee Boudreaux murmured, wiggling her three-year-old son Oliver's big toe. Oliver squealed with delight and tried to pull his foot away. Laughing, Aimee held onto his foot and grabbed the next toe. "This little piggy stayed back at the bayou."

Oliver giggled and squirmed, then cocked his head to the side and stuck his bottom lip out in a show of great sympathy. "Poor little piggy," he said sadly. "All alone."

Aimee dropped a light kiss onto the tip of his big toe. "Maman would never leave Oliver all alone by the bayou."

"No." Oliver shook his head solemnly. "And I never go there without you or Pépère."

"That's right." She tickled the tender underside of his foot, then caught his third toe. "This little piggy ate roast beef on french bread—"

"Batard! Fornicateur!"

Startled, Aimee lifted her head and turned in the direction of the expletives, toward her family's bait-and-tackle shop located just behind them. She drew her eyebrows together. Her father had a hot temper, and it wasn't unusual for him and a crony to all but come to blows over nothing more than a difference of opinion. At least, it wouldn't have been unusual before his illness. These days he rarely...

Another stream of angry French followed the first, and Aimee hurried to her feet. She held her hand out to Oliver. "Come on, baby. We better go check on your *pépère*. We'll finish our picnic and game later."

Oliver followed her up, his expression concerned. "Why's Pépère yelling?"

"I don't know, sweetheart," she said, starting for the store. "Why don't we—"

"Aimee!" her father shouted from inside the shop. "Bring me my shotgun! *Dépêche-toi!*"

Shotgun! Heart in her throat, Aimee scooped up Oliver and ran for the store. She bypassed the stairs, taking her father's ramp instead, and within moments was pulling open the screen door. She set Oliver down and motioned for him to stay put. "Papa!" she called, racing into the store. "What's wrong, what's happened..." She stopped in her tracks, her words dying on her tongue.

Hunter. It couldn't be.

But it was. He stood just inside the door, his expression frozen with alarm.

Aimee sucked in a steadying breath. Hunter had stolen her heart and the last of her youthful naïveté; he had given her the light of her life even as he had taught her that life rarely gave what one wished for. She'd once loved him as passionately as she'd later hated him.

She'd thought she would never see him again.

She drew in another deep breath. She'd always thought his looks part California surf bum, part serious intellectual. He had the slim, muscular body of the beach enthusiast, the perpetual golden tan, the California blond hair. She had loved running her fingers through his hair, thick and straight and like silken gold against her fingers.

His face and eyes spoke of a different kind of man. One who could be moody. One who contemplated. So many times she had found his ocean blue eyes upon her, intently studying, telling her nothing, but seeming to absorb everything. He'd always held himself slightly apart from the world, from her.

Instead of being put off by his reserve, his quiet intensity, she'd been drawn by it. And to the well of pain that reserve hid so well.

She'd been young, impossibly starry-eyed. She'd believed she could bring him out, change him, his life. But then she'd still believed that life was her own personal oyster, and that she could, by force of will alone, make all her dreams come true.

She'd been such a fool.

Aimee lifted her chin. That hadn't even been four years ago, but it might as well have been a lifetime. If he expected to find the open and willing girl whose heart he had so easily caught and crushed, he was in for a surprise.

Hunter turned to her then, slowly, cautiously, as if concerned over her father's next move. His gaze met hers and in that moment it seemed as if time stood still, as if the world retreated, leaving only the connection of their gazes. Vaguely, she heard her father mutter an oath, heard the quiet creak of his chair being galvanized into motion, saw him wheel to the storeroom.

Hunter hadn't changed in the three and a half years that had passed. Strange. When she looked into her own mirror, she saw so much change in herself. What would he see when he looked at her?

Hunter searched her expression. She wouldn't have expected anything less. "Hello, Aimee."

"Hunter."

"How are you?"

"Fine."

"Maman?" Oliver peeked around the corner. "Can I come now?"

Aimee turned to her son. She forced a calm smile. "It's fine, baby. Come on." She held out her arm and he scurried over to her and wrapped himself around her legs. She put a hand on his head, gently stroking, and returned her attention to Hunter. She arched her eyebrows. "What can I do for you?"

"No hello for an old friend?"

Old friend? Aimee thought, her heart turning over. She'd once loved him so desperately, she'd thought she would die without him. But then, he'd never felt the same about her. "No," she said simply. "Not now. Not after all this time."

"I'm sorry. I know I hurt you."

She stiffened. He'd always cut straight to the chase. There had been times she'd hated that about him. "Do you?"

"Yes."

She lifted her eyebrows in disbelief and Hunter cocked his head, his gaze moving from her to Oliver and back. "Handsome boy."

"Thank you." Aimee drew Oliver even closer to her. What, she wondered, did Hunter see when he looked at her son? Did he see anything of himself in the sturdy toddler? Certainly not in the eyes and hair, both the deep, rich brown of chocolate; not in the skin, darkened to bronze by the Louisiana sun. But, as she did, could Hunter see the resemblance of father and son in Oliver's face? In the big eyes that thoughtfully studied? In the small cleft that cut his chin? In the high, broad forehead?

Hunter studied Oliver. "How old is he?"

Aimee stiffened, tightening her hold on her son. The question made her feel threatened. Unreasonably, she told herself. Hunter had no interest in being a father.

Ignoring his question, she asked one of her own. "Why are you here, Hunter?"

He paused, and for the first time Aimee glimpsed his hesitation, his discomfort. That this meeting wasn't easy for him either tugged at her. She wished it didn't; when it had come to Hunter, she'd always been too empathic.

"This past week I attended a medical convention in New Orleans and I . . . thought of you. I wanted to see you." He looked away, then back. "I wanted to make sure you were . . . okay."

He'd thought of her? After three years, he wanted to make sure she was okay? The softening she'd felt toward him a moment before disappeared. "Well," she said coolly, "as you can see, I am. If there's nothing else, Oliver and I will get back to our picnic."

"*Are* you all right, Aimee?" He took a step toward her. "Are you really?"

His voice was low, intimate. Full of the kind of concern reserved for only those who had shared the most personal, private kind of relationship. It moved over her, pulling at her in ways she couldn't have imagined after all this time. She drew in a deep, steadying breath. "Why do you ask? Do I look sick, doctor?"

"No." He shook his head. "You look good. Beautiful, in fact. But you've . . . changed."

She stiffened. "It's been a long time."

"Yes, it has. Three and a half years."

Aimee curved her fingers possessively around Oliver's shoulder. "Well, you've seen me. You can go now."

Except for a flicker of emotion in his eyes, he appeared unaffected by her blunt words. "I don't blame you for being angry."

She understood suddenly. He'd come out of guilt.

Damn him, she thought angrily. She didn't want his guilt. She didn't want his regrets. She had enough of her own.

"You're a little late for that," she murmured. "I'm not angry. Not any more. So if you're after redemption, you're going to have to look elsewhere."

Her father wheeled back into the room, his shotgun across his lap. "Move aside, Aimee," he ordered. "Take my *petit-fils* back to his lunch."

"Papa?" She shook her head disbelievingly. "What are you doing?"

"This, it is between us men." He curled his big hands around the gun. "Go. Now."

She held up her own hands, trying to calm him. "Put the gun away. There's no need to—"

"Enough!" her father said, lifting the weapon and aiming it at Hunter's chest. "What do you plan to do by my Aimee?" he demanded, cocking the gun.

Aimee took another step toward her father. "This is ridiculous, Papa. Put the gun away." When he still didn't move, Aimee glared at him. "You don't understand."

He spared her a glance. "I may be old, *chère,* but some things, they are the same since forever." He narrowed his eyes once again on Hunter. "So, how do you plan to make it right by my Aimee and her *fils?* Or are you no better than the snakes that slither through the bayou?"

For a moment, the silence was deafening. Then Hunter looked from Aimee to Oliver, then back again. She could almost see the wheels turning in his head, putting two and two together. Stunned disbelief crossed his face. "Aimee?"

She cleared her throat. "Hunter, I—"

Disbelief became a dawning fury. "How old *is* he, Aimee? You never said."

Heart hammering, Aimee faced her father. His expression mirrored Hunter's. She cleared her throat again. "Papa, I can handle this. Please take Oliver outside."

Hunter caught her arm, his fingers circling her like bands of steel. As he did, her father lifted the shotgun again, and Hunter released her. "How could you...not have told me?"

Beginning to shake, she swung back to Hunter. She'd worried about this moment; she'd dreamed of it. She had never truly believed it would come. Now it was here, and she hadn't the faintest idea what to say.

"Oliver," she commanded, "take your *pépère* out to our picnic. Hurry, before the squirrels get our lunch."

He clung to her legs, obviously frightened. "You come, too."

Aimee's heart twisted. He'd picked up on her emotions, her alarm. How could he have not? She should have sent him from the room long ago. Guilt twisted through her. What else had he picked up in the last minutes?

Forcing a reassuring smile, she ruffled his hair. "I'll be out in a moment. Go on, baby. Everything's fine."

Giving her a hesitant glance, Oliver crossed to his grandfather. After leveling her an angry glance, Aimee's father let Oliver lead him out.

Watching them go, Aimee sighed. After Hunter, she would have to face her son's confusion and her father's anger—and disappointment.

As the screen door slammed shut, Aimee turned back to Hunter. His expression had lost all surprise and disbelief. All that remained was the anger. His eyes were dark with the emotion, his jaw tight with it.

"The boy is mine?" he asked, his voice tight.

"The *boy* has a name," she snapped, furious herself. At Hunter for having put her in this position in the first place, at his being here now. "Oliver."

"Is . . . he . . . mine?"

Aimee folded her arms across her chest. "Yes."

Swearing, Hunter swung away from her. For long moments, he stared at the doorway and the light that funnelled through the screen. She stared at his stiff back, the rigid line of his shoulders, the silence tautening between them as the seconds ticked past.

Finally, he swung back around, pinning her with his furious gaze. "How dare you, Aimee?"

"How dare I what?" she asked, jerking her chin up. "Get pregnant? It happens all the time, Hunter. Didn't you know?" She laughed without humor, her chest heavy and aching. "Especially to silly girls who have stars in their eyes."

"Give me a break!" He took a step closer to her, the movement almost menacing. "You were hardly a teenager. You weren't even a virgin."

She'd never seen him really angry; in all the time they'd spent together he'd never become more than annoyed. The emotion that emanated from him now was awesome, daunting. Drawing a deep breath, she held her ground even as instinct urged her to run. "Would it have changed anything if I had been?"

"Stop it. You were always so good at manipulating reality. Twisting it to fit your own perspective, your own needs." He curled his fingers into fists. "We're talking about why you kept your pregnancy a secret from me, about why you felt that was your right. Don't try to change this discussion into anything else."

"Fine." She met his gaze directly. "You made it clear you didn't want me. That you *never* wanted another child. What would have been the point of telling you I was pregnant?" She narrowed her eyes on him. "Or were you lying?"

"You know I wasn't."

His baldly spoken words weren't a surprise. They cut like a knife anyway. "I repeat, what would have been the point? I wasn't interested in trying to 'trap' you into a loveless marriage. I wasn't interested in hurting you or making you feel guilty."

Hunter made a sound of frustration. And fury. "Because it was my right to know."

"I didn't see it that way. I still don't."

"It took two, Aimee. Half of that child is me."

She took a step back, alarmed by his tone, the expression in his eyes. He couldn't want rights to Oliver. He couldn't, not this man who had professed never to want another child.

Aimee curled her fingers into fists. "Oliver is mine," she said softly but clearly. "It's always been just him and me. He's secure and happy. He would be confused if suddenly..." She took a deep, calming breath unable to even finish the thought. "If circumstances had been different, I would have told you. If I'd thought you had *any* interest in being a father again.

But I'd rather Oliver think he had no father, than one who didn't want him. I thought it would be better if you were unknown to him. I still do."

Hunter opened his mouth as if to protest, then shut it again. Pain, mixed with relief, spiraled through her. Relief that she could finally let go of the fear that someday Hunter would show up and demand rights to Oliver. Pain that he could have seen their son and not ache with love for him.

Aimee brought a hand to the back of her neck and rubbed wearily. "We're not doing each other any good here. We never did each other any good."

"Aimee, that's not true. I don't want you to—"

She shook her head, cutting off his words. "I'd like you to leave now. Whatever we had ended a long time ago." She started to walk away. "Have a nice life, Hunter Powell."

"Did I do this to you?" he asked softly, stopping her.

She looked back at him, meeting his eyes. In them was an expression she'd never seen before. "Do what?"

"Change you? Did I hurt you so badly?"

A dozen different emotions barreled through her. Hurt. Anger. Grief. The urge to cry. Before today, she'd thought she was over feeling anything for Hunter Powell, even anger. She flexed her fingers. Damn him for coming back, for stirring up memories best forgotten, for rekindling past pain.

"Did I, Aimee?" he asked again.

Yes, she wanted to shout. You hurt me so badly I thought I would never be whole again. Instead, she shook her head and met his eyes evenly. "You give yourself way too much credit, Hunter. *Au revoir.*"

She turned and walked away, not wanting to afford him the opportunity to answer, knowing that another moment would bring tears. He called her name again, softly, and she held her breath, wondering if he would come after her, torn between hoping he would and praying he wouldn't.

He didn't.

A cry caught in her throat as she heard the shop's screen door slam. A moment later she heard an engine roar to life, followed by the sound of tires on the shell drive.

She swallowed. No surprises—Hunter never had come after her. This was for the best; it was what she wanted.

Aimee drooped against the doorjamb, needing its support. She sucked in a shuddering breath, willing her legs and arms to stop shaking. Willing her heart to slow and her tears to dry.

After all this time, why had he come? Why couldn't he have left well enough alone? Time had healed her. She'd finally put the past behind her. She'd gone on.

Now, he'd reopened the wound. How long would it take it to close this time? A week? A month? Years, again?

Aimee brought a trembling hand to her mouth. For so long, she'd fantasized him coming after her, declaring his love, telling her that he couldn't live without her. When those fantasies had died, she'd created others, ones where she'd been cool and unaffected by his pleas and promises, ones where she hurt him the way he'd hurt her.

In her head, she had prepared what she would say to him, had rehearsed how she would act and react. Always in her fantasies, she'd bested him.

And then there'd been nothing. She'd let go. Of the fantasies. The hurt. The love.

Aimee laughed softly, the sound wrenched from a place somewhere deep inside of her. She hadn't had a clue. Every part of her had been affected by seeing him. And as it had always been between them, it had been Hunter who was cool. Hunter who had been unaffected.

Aimee stared through the screen door, out at her father and Oliver, sitting together under the shade of the huge, old oak. Its thick, twisted branches, draped with spanish moss, stretched out over the yard, providing shade but blocking the sun so that little grass grew beneath.

She could tell by the rigid line of her father's shoulders that he was furious with her. He wouldn't understand why she'd lied to him—or rather, he would see what she'd told him as a lie. She didn't. She'd told her father that Hunter had been married, that he hadn't wanted anything to do with her or Oliver. Neither had been a lie, for although Hunter's wife was dead, he had been still very much married to her.

Aimee brushed impatiently at the tears that slipped down her cheeks. So now she'd hurt her father again. Disappointed him again. It seemed she'd made a life out of doing both.

Oliver looked anxiously up at the store; she heard him ask his *pépère* for her. She drew in another steadying breath, then released it. She would have time for tears, for self-recriminations, later. Her son needed her.

She pushed through the door and headed across the lawn. "Did you save Mommy any lunch?" she called, forcing a bright smile.

"Maman!" Oliver jumped up and raced toward her, his face radiating love.

He launched himself at her and she swung him into her arms, hugging him tightly. "Hi, baby. Are you and Pépère having fun?"

Oliver nodded and snuggled against her. She breathed in his sweet scent, part baby still and part boy already, and her heart turned over. What would she do if she lost him? She kissed his silky head. "I love you."

"Love, too." He wound his fingers, sticky with grape jelly, in her hair. "That man gone?"

"Mmm-hmm." She pressed her nose to his. "He was just an old friend, baby. He won't be coming back."

Her father made a gruff sound and she dared a glance at him. He sent her a dark look, one filled with questions and accusations.

"Not now, Papa," she murmured, hearing the tremor in her own voice and cursing it. "Oliver needs his nap. We'll talk later."

Without a word, her father turned away from her and began to wheel slowly back to the store. Her chest heavy with unshed tears, Aimee watched him go.

Several miles up the road Hunter stood at the edge of the bayou, staring out at the dark water. He had a son. Dear Lord, he was a father. Again. The thing he had promised himself would never happen had happened without his even knowing it.

A son. Hunter pressed the heels of his shaking hands against his eyes, memories of another toddler, another son, bursting through his head like fireworks, obliterating everything but the pain of the memories. Unlike Aimee's boy, Pete had been fair. Tow-headed, with huge blue eyes. He'd been tall for his age and full of mischief. He hadn't had the seriousness of Aimee's son, nor the clinginess.

He and Ginny had adored Pete. He'd been the center of their universe. And Pete had basked in that love as only a baby can—unshakably and without questions, confident in himself and his world.

Hunter squeezed his eyes shut. If he dug deeply into his well of memories he could hear Pete's baby voice in his head. *"I love you, Daddy."* Digging deeper, he could feel those chubby little arms around his neck, hugging, could feel his child's weight in his arms, against his chest.

"But why can't we go, Daddy? I'll be a good boy."

Hunter sucked in a sharp breath, the pain sawing through him like a jagged, dull blade. His vision blurred, and he swore. At the heavens, at hell. It was so senseless. Why Pete? Why his bright, beautiful little boy? There were so few miracles in this world and so much ugliness. His little boy had been a miracle. His little boy had been light and love and goodness.

And what of Ginny? Hunter clenched his fingers into fists of futility and frustration. Sweet, gentle, kind to everyone. What had she done to deserve her fate? What had been the purpose of taking her?

Her voice rang in his head. "Don't worry, sweetheart. We'll be fine. Don't forget, I love you."

Forget. If only he could. Lord knew, for almost five years now he'd tried. The best he'd been able to do was bury the memories, never digging into the well, never probing, refusing to remember.

But pain had a way of seeking one out, memories of slipping through cracks—despite steel-willed resolutions, despite desperate promises.

Hunter swung his gaze once more to the water, forcibly dragging himself back from the depths. He breathed deeply through his nose, the memories ebbing, taking the pain with them, leaving only emptiness behind. And cold. A numbing, killing cold.

He brushed impatiently at his cheeks, at the moisture there, focusing on the scents and sounds of the bayou. The scents ranged from unbearably sweet to citrus sharp, each hauntingly potent. Magnolia, he'd guess; mimosa and sweet olive he recognized. The sounds were subtler—the rustle of the lush vegetation, the plop of a frog or turtle sliding into the water, the shrill call of a cicada.

Hunter moved closer to the water. His first impression of this place, of Aimee's world, had been of water and a green that went on forever. And of life. Vibrant. Throbbing. Sexual. The way Aimee had been when she'd first come into his life.

He'd never forgotten what it had been like touching her, making love to her. Would it be the same now? he wondered, watching as an egret burst into flight.

Would Aimee's touch, her taste, move him the way it
had back then? Would he still feel guilt at that cata-
clysmic reaction to her—a reaction such as he'd never
experienced with another woman, not even with
Ginny?

In the years that had passed, Aimee's looks had
richened, matured. Like a flower in full bloom, her
curves were softer, more lush, her face stamped now
with something sensual, something that looked more
like a woman and less like a girl. In truth, impossibly,
she was even more beautiful now than she'd been then.

But she'd changed in other ways as well. Ways that
weren't as soft, ways that disturbed him. Hunter bent
and picked up a small stone. He held it in his hand,
weighing it, rubbing his fingers over it, finding its surface subtly scarred. Gone was the girl who had sucked
him into her whirlwind of reckless joie de vivre. The
girl who had rushed headlong, willfully even, toward
her future. The girl who had given him a few stunning
months of reflective warmth.

She was harder now. She had an edge—one that
could cut. Not that there wasn't any softness there—he
saw it in the way she looked at her son, the way she
spoke to her father. But the Aimee he'd known hadn't
had the capacity for cynicism, for sarcasm. Only for
laughter and daring—sometimes misplaced, sometimes foolish, but she was always likable. Always honest.

Hunter felt a moment of sorrow, of grief, for the girl
she had been. And a stab of guilt. Because he knew
he'd been at least partly responsible for her departure.
He supposed he shouldn't feel guilty. He'd told her up

front that he didn't have anything to offer her, that there would never be a happily-ever-after for them. But that didn't change the fact that he'd hurt her, that he'd gotten her pregnant.

Reeling back, Hunter flung the stone toward the bayou. It struck the glassy surface and sent shock waves rippling over the quiet water in ever widening circles.

He was responsible. He had responsibility. To her. To her son.

Turning, Hunter started back to his rental car. Like it or not, he was a father. Oliver was his. He didn't doubt Aimee's word; she wouldn't lie. It wasn't in her. *That,* he was certain, hadn't changed.

He understood why she hadn't told him about Oliver. He didn't want to understand, but he did. And if he was being brutally honest with himself, and he might as well be, he'd been angrier about the fact he had a son than about her secrecy.

But now he did know about Oliver and he couldn't turn his back on her or the boy. That wasn't in him. He would offer her financial support; he would insist she take it. He owed her that much.

Hunter unlocked the car door, then slipped inside. Aimee wouldn't be happy to see him again; he would go back anyway. It was the least—and the most—he could do.

Chapter Two

Hunter found Aimee alone in the store. She stood behind the counter, counting the money in the cash drawer. She didn't hear him enter and he stopped just inside the door. Moving his gaze over her, he used the moment to study her as he'd been unable to earlier.

She wore a plain white T-shirt and a pair of denim cutoffs. She'd dressed in a similar fashion when she'd lived in California, never being one for airs or following the pack. He'd always admired that—and he'd always thought she looked sensational. There was something infinitely sexy about a woman who knew who she was and dressed accordingly.

Hunter tipped his head. As she worked, her thick, straight hair slipped over her shoulder and fell across her face, like a dark, silky waterfall. She reached up and tucked the strands back behind her ear and he recalled doing the same for her many times, recalled how those heavy strands had felt against his own fingers.

Awareness moved over him and Hunter breathed deeply through his nose. A scent drifted on the air, rich and spicy, stirred by the ceiling fan that whirled above. He smiled, the smell bringing back memories of the times he and Aimee had spent in the kitchen cooking, of the times food had been forgotten in favor of other, more urgent hungers.

Hunter's thoughts jerked back to the present as Aimee sighed and dumped the pennies back into the drawer. His chest tightened at the sound, a combination of frustration, fatigue and futility. He had no doubt that his appearance played a big, maybe even exclusive, role in bringing about that sound.

He stepped forward. "Aimee?"

The nickels slipped from her fingers, clattering into the metal drawer. She looked up, meeting his eyes. In hers he read surprise and hesitation. And a glimmer of something sad; something akin to her sigh.

She rested her hands on the cash drawer. "I thought we said goodbye."

She'd meant the words to be hard, but they were soft. Unbearably so. He moved farther into the room. "I couldn't leave. Not that way, not before..." He cleared his throat. "I want to give you some support. Financial support. For Oliver."

She snapped the drawer shut and swung around to face him fully. "We're doing just fine without any...help. Thank you, but no."

He took another step toward her. "A college fund, then."

She shook her head, her dark hair swinging with the movement, brushing her shoulders. "No."

Hunter lowered his gaze for a moment, fighting frustration and annoyance, reminding himself to consider this from Aimee's standpoint. "I understand your concern. I was a...parent once, too. And the last thing I would want is for Oliver to be hurt because of me. But he never has to know where the money came from. We can—"

"No." Aimee came out from behind the counter and crossed to the light switch. She laid her hand on the plate and met his eyes evenly. "I'm closing up now."

Hunter drew his eyebrows together. "Why are you being so obstinate?"

"I don't think I'm being obstinate. There's no sense taking what we don't need. We're doing fine. Now, I really need to go check on my gumbo."

She smiled, trying to reassure him. Hunter wasn't fooled; the curving of her lips was stiff, forced. He had the sudden sense that she was terrified.

He looked around them at the rustic store, with its conglomeration of goods, everything from fishing tackle to homemade candies and crafts, to cold drinks and snacks. Was this their sole means of support?

The building itself was unpretentious, sturdy. Constructed of cypress clapboard with a high pitched roof and a gallery that ran the length of the building, it looked as if it had been built to withstand the worst that nature could dish up.

He remembered the way her father looked, with his weathered face, its road map of folds and creases defining a man who had worked hard all his life. A man who had taken care of his family. Hunter admired that; he respected people who could live simply and with little more than what nature provided. Especially in these modern, high-tech times.

But what if Oliver wanted more?

Aimee saw his gaze, and she stiffened her spine. "We do fine, Hunter. You don't need to feel guilty or responsible—"

"But I am responsible."

She sighed; again the sound tore at him. He crossed to her. "I can afford this, Aimee. I want to do it."

She tipped up her chin. "It wouldn't even make a dent. Right?"

"You know it wouldn't."

She turned away from him. "I don't want your guilt money," she said softly. "I don't want the least you can do."

He caught her arm, forcing her to turn her face to his. He searched her gaze. "Then, what do you want?"

For one long moment, she said nothing. He could see the pulse that beat wildly at the base of her throat, felt the shudder that rippled over her. Whether these were reactions to fear or awareness he wasn't sure.

"Nothing," she said finally, softly. "I want nothing from you except for you to leave me—us—alone."

The words stung and he fought to hold on to the control, the unflappable logic, that had served him so well for so long. "You're letting your emotions talk. Think, Aimee. Oliver might want to go to Harvard some day. Or Juilliard. Or Cal Tech. Who knows? This would give him the opportunity to make his dreams come true." He lowered his voice. "You had dreams, Aimee. Remember?"

She jerked her arm from his grasp, furious. She clenched her fingers into fists. "I'll find a way. On my own. Besides, he might choose to stay and live like the Cajun people have for generations."

"You didn't."

"I was wrong to want to leave. It was a mistake." She glared at him. "And we aren't talking about me."

"Aren't we?" He moved toward her again, until she had nowhere to look but at him. "I don't think you were wrong. You were better than merely good. Your photographs were special. You were a real talent."

Giving in to the urge, he reached out and touched her flushed cheek. Her skin was warm and impossibly soft against his fingers. He remembered a time when he'd had the freedom to touch her like this whenever he chose, then he cursed the memory. But still he didn't draw away his hand. "What happened to your dreams, Aimee? What about your photography?"

"I'm just a bayou bumpkin," she whispered. "Remember? Isn't that what the critics called me?"

"They were wrong." He moved his hand, threading his fingers through her hair. "You're a gifted artist."

She looked away, catching her bottom lip between her teeth.

Her self-doubt tore at him; Hunter reminded himself that it was neither his place to comfort or reassure. He'd come back for one reason only—Oliver. He dropped his hand. "I want to do this," he murmured. "Think of Oliver. Give him this chance."

"Think of Oliver?" she repeated, meeting his gaze once more. Her dark eyes flashed with fury. "What do you think I do all day, all night?" She pushed away from him, her breathing ragged with her anger. "How dare you waltz in here and tell me how to care for my son! How dare you presume to tell me what my son might need or want."

Hunter swore. "Aimee, I didn't mean to imply you weren't a good mother or that you weren't looking after his needs."

"No? Then what are you doing? He means nothing to you, Hunter. Nothing." She pressed her hands to her chest. "But he means everything to me. I love him so much I . . ."

She shook her head, choking back the thoughts. "I don't want him hurt. And if I take your money, someday he will find out about you. Someday he'll know you didn't want him."

The words, the truth in them, clawed at Hunter in a way he didn't understand but still felt on an elemental level. He wasn't accustomed to confusion; emotion was an anathema to him. Now, he was stewing in both. He swore again. "I can't leave it this way. I won't."

"Why?" she asked, her voice high and tight. "For God's sake, yesterday you didn't even know Oliver existed and you were fine. He was fine. What's so different now? Just go back to California. Just forget about today, forget about us."

"I can't," he said simply. "Knowing changes everything."

For long moments she said nothing, just stared at the window and the fading light of the day. Finally, she turned back to him, tears sparkling in her eyes. "I don't understand," she whispered, catching his hands, pleading with him. "Why, Hunter? Why can't you just let this go?"

He curled his fingers around hers, holding on to her in a way that surprised him. In a way that was too intimate for the strangers they had become. But even knowing that, he didn't let go.

He looked down at their joined hands, then back up at her, an unfamiliar tightness in his chest. "I don't completely understand myself. But I can't. He's my son. I can't love him—but I won't abandon him, either."

Aimee made a sound of pain and frustration. She released his hands and wheeled away from him. "How can you abandon something, someone, you never had?"

"That wasn't my choice, Aimee. It was yours."

"I'm not going to change my mind," she said stiffly, facing him again.

"Then the ball's in my court, isn't it?" Hunter let out a sharp breath, totally frustrated. "You're not leaving me many options."

"No, I'm not."

For long moments, Hunter gazed at her. Then, muttering an oath, he crossed to the door and swung it open.

"Goodbye, Hunter," she said softly.

He looked back at her, furious. That she'd thwarted him. That he felt so damn guilty. So torn. He fought to keep his voice cool and unaffected. "What makes you think this is goodbye?"

Hunter let himself out, shutting the screen gently behind him. As he swung away from the door, he saw that Aimee's father waited for him. The old man sat next to the rental car, blocking the driver's side door. He sat quietly in the fading sun, his big hands resting on the chair's arms. Hunter was relieved to see he'd left his shotgun behind.

Hunter descended the stairs. Three and a half years ago Aimee had described her father as vital and fit, an outdoorsman who hunted, fished and shrimped for a living. She'd also called him crusty and opinionated, a man very much wedded to the old ways. A man who resisted change.

Yet the man before him now was much changed from the one Aimee had described. At least physically. By the slight drooping of his right eye, Hunter suspected Roubin Boudreaux was the victim of an aneurysm. He wondered when it had happened.

Roubin turned and looked directly at Hunter as he approached. Once again Hunter thought of pride. "You and me," Roubin said, "we have some unfinished business."

"It seems that way," Hunter murmured, stopping before Roubin, leaving enough distance between them so the older man wouldn't have to bend his neck back to meet his eyes.

"My Aimee, she is a stubborn girl."

"She takes after you, I suspect."

Roubin chuckled, the sound rich with age. "But we Cajuns, we would not have made it so far if we were not so." Roubin shook his head and lifted a gnarled finger. "But you, *mon ami,* you are not innocent in this matter. *Non.*"

"No," Hunter agreed, the truth of that twisting in his gut.

"You are prepared to make this matter right?"

"As best I can." Hunter made a sound of frustration. "It's complicated."

Roubin raised his eyebrows, mocking him. "Not so complicated, eh? You have a son."

"I love you, daddy."

Hunter drew in a sharp breath. "It appears that way."

"I hear Aimee, what she says to you in there." Roubin shook his head again. "Sometimes, my Aimee, she is too emotional as well as too stubborn." The older man lifted his face to the sky as a bobwhite called out above them, then turned back to Hunter, his gaze thoughtful. "And I think, too, you hurt her very much."

Hunter thought again of the woman Aimee had been and the one she had become. And of his own part in that transformation. Remorse curled through him. And guilt. "It wasn't intentional."

"But only a monster sets out to hurt another."

"Look..." Hunter made a sound of frustration. "...I'm not giving up. I intend to make amends for this situation. Aimee refused my help, so I'm going to have to come up with something. I'm just not sure what."

Roubin paused, then as if coming to a decision slapped his hand on the chair arm. "There is a room at the back of the store. I sometimes rent her to hunters.

She is clean, the bed is firm. I will rent her to you until this matter is resolved. Fifty dollars a week, meals included."

Hunter heard the screen door open and looked up. Aimee stood there, her cheeks bright with anger. Without a doubt she had heard her father's offer, just as certainly she wanted him to refuse it.

Hunter looked back at Roubin. He would have to make arrangements with his partners, would have to have the other doctors cover his patient load. There would be appointments to be canceled and rescheduled, a handful of events and meetings that could not be rescheduled. It would be damn difficult.

Hunter nodded. "Thank you. Yes, I would very much appreciate the room. I'll get my things in New Orleans and be back tonight."

"Bon." Roubin nodded and rolled his chair away from the car so Hunter could open the door.

Aimee watched as Hunter climbed into the car, started it and drove off. When it had disappeared from sight, she turned to her father. She curled her fingers into fists. "How could you?" she asked. "You know how I feel."

He met her gaze solemnly. "But how could I know, *chère?*"

Aimee lowered her eyes. "I didn't lie to you, Papa. Not really."

"Not really?" He laughed without humor. "There is truth and there is untruth. Black or white. So, *chère,* which did you tell me when you came back home?"

She and her father had seldom seen eye-to-eye. Why had she expected anything different now? "It's not always that way, Papa. Not this time."

"Oh?" He maneuvered his chair around to face her fully. "So, tell me. How can you call this not black, not white?"

She took a deep, painful breath. She didn't know which hurt more, recounting the past or facing her father this way. She stalled the inevitable one more moment. "Shall I wheel you up?"

He nodded, and she descended the ramp, then pushed him slowly up to the gallery. "Oliver is still with his cousins?" she asked.

"*Oui.*"

"Good." Aimee leaned against one of the gallery's unadorned cypress columns and stared out at the gathering dusk. After a moment, she murmured, "Hunter *was* married. He had a child. A boy. His son and his wife died."

"A great tragedy."

"Yes." Aimee turned away from her father, not wanting him to see the tears in her eyes. She rested her head against the column. "I told you he was a married man because he was in his heart, Papa. He still loved her. He was never able to let her go. Or his son."

She shook her head, her eyes brimming, feeling like an idiot. And like a daughter who had disgraced her father. "He didn't want me for his own, he didn't love me. He was very up front and honest about that. He never tried to lead me on, never tried to trick me."

She did look at her father then. "But I refused to believe what he told me. I fooled myself into believing he would fall in love with me. Eventually. Then I learned I was pregnant.''

She laughed, the sound shaky and sad even to her own ears. ''I was certain everything was going to be fine. I still thought I could make him...love me. I thought that once he knew about the baby he would change. After all, he had adored his first son.''

Her father drew his heavy eyebrows together. ''But you didn't tell him?''

She curved her fingers around the column. ''No.''

''*Bon Dieu!* Why?''

Aimee brushed at the tears that spilled over. How could she explain that time in her life to her father? He'd forbidden her to leave La Fin, had insisted she belonged with her people. In fact, before she'd left he'd told her that until she returned, ready to do her duty to him and her people, she would be dead to him. She'd defied him, not believing he meant what he said. Convinced that he would come around, that she could make him come around.

Just as she hadn't believed Hunter when he'd told her he would never love her; just as she'd been sure Hunter would come around.

She'd been so ridiculously naive.

Aimee drew in a deep breath, looking once more at her father. ''I didn't tell him because I finally saw what he'd been telling me all along. He was never going to love me. He wouldn't want the baby. All my telling him would have done was make him feel guilty and trapped. I didn't want either. I still don't.''

''You were wrong, *chère.*'' Her father shook his head. ''A man should know the consequences of his actions. A man should be given the opportunity to be a man. To take care of what's his. To take care of his family.''

"That's why you invited him here?" she asked incredulously. "Because you think he should take care of me and Oliver?" She couldn't believe he would want that. Her father had always been as proud as he was independent.

"There is only one way to take care of your family.''

He thought Hunter would marry her, Aimee realized, stunned. He thought it Hunter's obligation. His duty. Her father believed that if Hunter was a man, a real man, he would see that and do the correct thing. He'd offered Hunter the room as a nudge in the proper direction.

"Oh, Papa... you don't understand. Today, things like this happen all the time. Today, many women raise children alone. Besides, even if Hunter offered, I don't love him any more. And I'd never want a man out of obligation or a sense of duty.''

Roubin scowled at her. "I'm so old-fashioned, eh? So out of date with my old ways? Maybe you should throw me in the swamp and let the gators fight over me.''

Aimee bent down in front of his chair and gathered his hands in hers. "His wife and son died. Horribly. He'll never marry. He'll never have another child. He won't, Papa.''

"You're wrong, *chère*." Roubin smiled and squeezed her hands. "He has another child. A fine, strong boy.''

His simplistic view of life infuriated her. It always had. "And what about Oliver?" she demanded. "This could hurt him. This *will* hurt him."

"He's already hurt. He needs a father."

Guilt sawed through her, and she looked away. "He has you. All the relatives. He's very well loved. You've only to look at him to see how happy he is."

"He is young yet."

Aimee let her breath out in a frustrated huff. "Fine. We're not going to agree on this. You've rented the room to Hunter, and he will come and stay. But I'm not going to change my mind, Papa."

She tried to stand. Roubin tightened his fingers on hers, stopping her. "I'm no role model for Oliver," he said sadly. "Maybe once, but no more. And the relatives? They come and they go. Oliver, he needs a man around day in an' out. He needs a man he can count on. A man who can teach him what he needs to know."

She curled her fingers around her father's, his skin hard and callused from the years of working with them. "He *can* count on you, Papa. Everything a man should be you can teach him."

Roubin shook his head, his expression growing bitter. And angry. "Look at me. I'm taken care of by women. I sell junk for tourists in my store. Once, I would have been out there with the men." He motioned to the bayou. "Once, I brought home food for the table."

Aimee lifted his hands to her cheek, hating his unhappiness. His bitterness. It hurt to hear him this way. "Dr. Landry says you could walk again. He says with hard work you could—"

"Walk with a cane," Roubin interrupted, his cheeks flushed. "At best. Not well enough to hunt or fish. Not well enough to take care of my family, the way a man should."

Their argument was a familiar one. Despite his doctor's recommendations and her own urging, her father refused to do the exercises necessary to progress. He refused to even try.

"But," she murmured, "you'd have some mobility. Wouldn't that be good? Look how far you've come since your—"

"It would have been better if the aneurysm, she had taken me."

"Don't say that!" Tears flooded her eyes. "I love you. Oliver loves you. Without you, I don't know what I would have done, or how I would have made it. You're strong, Papa, you hold us together as you always have. Without you . . ."

Roubin slipped his hands from hers and cupped her face. "Non. You never needed me, *chère*. Even when you were a *petit bébé,* you stood on your own two feet. You look me in the eye always."

"No, Papa, I—"

He shook his head, then pressed his lips to her forehead. "Oliver will be home soon and hungry. Come. The gumbo, she is sure to be ready."

Chapter Three

It was late when Hunter arrived back at Aimee's. He'd had to check out of the hotel and make a call to the clinic. His assistant had been surprised; they'd all expected him back the following morning. He hadn't explained, had only asked her to make arrangements with the other doctors to juggle his patient load, cancel his business appointments and his plane reservation. All indefinitely.

He could tell she thought he'd lost his mind. Truthfully, he wasn't so sure he hadn't.

Hunter climbed from the car, bringing the carefully packed music box with him. The night was still, the air heavy with moisture and thick with the sounds and smells of the bayou. Rounding the car to the trunk, he took out his garment bag and hiked it over his shoulder.

About forty yards toward the bayou from the store stood another building, its high pitched-roof construction the same as the first's. Aimee's home. Where she'd grown up, where she lived now with her father and son.

Hunter started toward it. In the light of day he had seen that it was bigger than the store, and homey. Flowers spilled from window boxes, the gallery was graced with a swing on one side of the front door and two highback rocking chairs on the other. Beside the house, a large vegetable garden was laid out.

Hunter's lips lifted. Aimee had always had a green thumb. She'd moved into his house and promptly filled every table, ledge and corner with plants. She'd made his garden her own personal project and had even shown the gardener a thing or two about making things grow.

After she'd left the plants had withered, then died. Within a month of her departure, the tables, ledges and corners were once again empty, green replaced by sterile white.

Hunter shook his head, annoyed with his thoughts. He hadn't expected seeing Aimee to trigger this melancholy trip down memory lane. He hadn't expected indecision. Or confusion. Or this overwhelming, irrational feeling of responsibility and protectiveness.

But of course, he hadn't expected to find he had a son.

A few lights burned inside the cottage and Hunter wondered if it was Aimee who waited up for him.

Probably. His chest tightened with anticipation and he swore under his breath. What they'd shared had been wonderful but brief. It was best for Aimee that it had ended. He wasn't here to mess up her life again.

He paused at the bottom of the stairs, gazing up at the long gallery, bathed in shadows. Taking a determined breath, he climbed the few steps and crossed to the door.

"You're scowling."

Startled, Hunter stopped and turned toward the darkest part of the gallery. Aimee sat on the porch swing, her knees drawn to her chest, a coffee mug cupped in her palms. Although he couldn't see her expression, he sensed anger. And sadness.

It was the latter that pulled at him more. He swore again, this time silently. "Was I?" he asked.

"Yes." She brought the mug to her lips and sipped. "If you're so unhappy about being here, why don't you leave?"

"I can't. We've already been through this."

She frowned. "That we have."

He closed the distance between them, stopping in front of her. "I'm sorry, Aimee."

She tipped her head back and met his eyes. "Are you?"

"Yes." He looked away, then back. "I know you don't want me here. But I have to do this."

"So you've said." She set her mug down sharply, and stood. "I'll show you to your room."

She brushed by him; he caught her arm. She met his eyes almost defiantly. He picked up the faintest whiff of her perfume, subtle and sweetly spicy. It swamped his senses now as it had back then, as it had the night they'd met.

The night they met. Their first meeting had been one of those chance encounters, two people coming together who—under normal circumstances—never would have met. He'd only gone to the art opening because Ginny had admired and collected the artist's work; he'd intended to duck in and duck out. Then he had run into a loquacious colleague.

While talking to the other doctor, he'd caught sight of Aimee from across the room. She'd been laughing, charming jaded jet-set art types who were never charmed. There had been something different about her, something special. Something brilliantly alive.

In a room full of people all striving to be unique, she'd seemed the only one who was.

He'd watched her, had been drawn to her, even. He'd had no plans to introduce himself, had had no interest in a woman other than Ginny.

But then she'd turned suddenly, and their eyes had met. She'd smiled; he'd smiled back.

And he'd been lost.

Or maybe it had been *she* who'd been lost.

"Hunter?" Aimee tugged against his grasp.

He blinked, the present coming into focus once more. He lowered his hand so his fingers circled her wrist. Her pulse thundered beneath his touch.

"Remember the night we met?" he asked, his voice husky with the memory.

Aimee hesitated a moment, then nodded. "Of course. Why?"

"I was thinking of that night. Of you and me and...fate." He rubbed his fingers rhythmically across the translucent flesh of her wrist. "We never should have met. We almost didn't."

For long seconds silence stretched between them. She cleared her throat. "I can't say that, Hunter. I can't even think it. How could I? If we hadn't met, I wouldn't have Oliver. And I love him more than anything."

Aimee slipped her hand from his and crossed the gallery to the stairs. She descended them and started across the yard toward the store. Hunter watched her go, pain and memories colliding inside him.

"I love you, Daddy."

"I love you, too, Pete. More than anything."

Hunter put his free hand on a cypress column, his legs suddenly shaky.

Pete giggled. "More than chocolate milk?"

"You bet, buddy. More than pizza, even."

"Then why can't I go, too? I'll be a good boy, Daddy. I promise."

"Hunter? Are you okay?"

Aimee stood several yards from the house, gazing quizzically up at him. He looked blankly at her, seeing for a moment Pete instead. He sucked in a sharp breath, his chest so tight the action hurt. He nodded and forced a stiff smile. "Fine. Just . . . fine."

He descended the steps and caught up with her in two strides.

They crossed the yard in silence. When they reached the other building, Aimee led him to a small porch on its far right side. They climbed the stairs and crossed to the door. She opened it, then handed him the key.

They both stepped inside. The room Roubin had rented him was simple and sparsely furnished, but nice. The furniture consisted of a double bed, small chest of drawers, an old wing chair, reading table and lamp. A small bathroom adjoined the room. As with the store, the room wasn't air-conditioned and the windows were all thrown wide to let in the cool night air; a ceiling fan whirled lazily above. A stack of fresh linens waited on the unmade bed.

"Is this yours?" Hunter asked, crossing to a black-and-white photo that hung on the wall by the chair.

"Yes."

He moved closer to the image, studying it. The photograph depicted a bayou immersed in a ghostly, billowing fog. The effect was haunting. Unforgettable. "It's beautiful."

"Thank you," she murmured, gazing at the photo. "I took that a long time ago."

Hunter drew his eyebrows together, studying her. Did she have any idea how wistful her expression was right now? Did she realize how much her eyes told him? He suspected not. For if she did, she would work harder to hide her feelings. This Aimee was not as open as the one he'd known all those years ago; this Aimee preferred to erect barriers around herself.

Was she this way with everyone? he wondered. Or just with him?

Aimee looked away, her wistfulness disappearing. "You'll be called for meals, but we eat around eight, noon and five. If you miss one, you're on your own."

Hunter set the music box on the table and laid his garment bag on the bed. "Fair enough."

"If you need something, just ask."

"I will."

"Good." She took a step toward the door, then stopped as she reached it. "I guess I'll see you in the morning."

"I guess so."

Aimee pushed open the screen door, then paused again. She turned back to him, making a small sound of annoyance as she did. "Isn't there any way I can talk you out of this?"

"Afraid not."

"What do you hope to accomplish here?" She folded her arms across her chest. "We've already agreed to disagree."

He unpacked the music box and carefully lifted it from its bed of tissue. He gazed at it a moment, thinking of what the saleswoman had said about going with one's gut. A smile tugged at his mouth, and he met Aimee's gaze. "I'm going to make you see things my way."

"And I already told you, you're not."

"Your father was right." Hunter gave in and smiled. "You are stubborn. I can't believe I didn't notice that before."

She scowled. "Stuff it, Powell."

Hunter lifted his eyebrows and laughed. "Stuff it? Exactly where did you have in mind, Ms. Boudreaux?"

For a moment it looked as if she were going to laugh. It pulled at her mouth, lit her eyes. In that moment he was reminded even more keenly of the girl she had been and of their time together.

The blood began to thrum in his head. He wanted to kiss her. Wanted to kiss her until they both forgot everything but the feel of each other's mouths, forgot everything but the need for even deeper, more intimate contact. He wanted them to lose themselves in each other, the way they used to.

Aimee saw his look. Her breath caught, the tiny sound reverberating in the quiet room. The blood rushed to her head; a place much lower began to throb. She hadn't been touched by a man in so long. She hadn't been looked at as a woman, a woman with needs, in forever.

The way Hunter looked at her now.

Aimee put a hand out behind her, bracing herself on the doorjamb. When was the last time she had been something other than a mother or daughter? When was the last time she had acknowledged her own needs? The last time she had allowed herself to be a woman?

She didn't need to ask herself the question. She knew the answer already. Three and a half years ago.

She lowered her eyes to Hunter's mouth, then skimmed them lower, across his chest and flat abdomen, lower still. She remembered what he'd looked like naked—lean and muscular and all male. She remembered how his flesh had felt beneath her fingers—firm but resilient, hot when aroused.

Longing raced through her, heat followed.

"Aimee," he murmured, his voice thick. He took a step nearer to her.

Stunned, she lifted her gaze back to his. What was she doing? She didn't love him any more. She didn't.

But love didn't have a thing to do with what she was feeling. Her body had always reacted to him this way. From the night they met, it had taken nothing more than a look, a word or smile, to send her into his arms, his bed.

She jerked her chin up. That was a long time ago. A lifetime even. She was no longer so naive. So easily impressed.

"If you've come here because you thought you and I could resume . . . or if you thought we could just pick up—"

"Where we left off?" he filled in, shaking his head. "It never crossed my mind."

She folded her arms across her chest and wished she could read something of his thoughts in his eyes. "Then, stop it."

"What? All I'm doing is looking at you."

That was enough. And that was the problem. "Then, it's what you're thinking. What you're remembering."

Hunter laughed and took another step toward her; she inched backward, hating that she had to tip her head back to meet his eyes. "Maybe it is. But some thoughts can't be stopped. They just . . . come."

He took another step. He was so close now she could feel his breath fan against her cheek. She fought the sensations that raced, lightninglike, over her.

"And the truth is," he murmured, lifting his hand to her face, his tone full of regret, "I never forgot touching you. Making love with you. I wanted to. Believe me, I tried.''

Aimee drew in a shuddering breath. Dear, God, she had tried, too. And been unsuccessful.

He moved his fingers lightly against her cheek. Aimee held absolutely still, torn between running for safety and the pleasure of his touch. She felt as if she had died and been reborn. Life, awareness, sprang from a place deep inside her; a small sigh wrenched from that same space.

The breath shuddered past Hunter's lips. ''This is going to be tough, Slick. A lot tougher than I thought.''

Slick. It had been his nickname for her. They had laughed over it because she had been anything but. Now, hearing it hurt. It brought all the foolishness she'd felt—over her silly dreams of Hunter and her own future and invincibility—scrambling to the surface.

The tender place inside her snapped closed; anger rushed over her in a cold, galvanizing wave.

She jerked away from his touch, reminding herself of the months of pain she had endured after their separation, of the months spent wishing—praying—Hunter would come after her. Reminding herself that Hunter wanted neither her nor their son.

''If it's going to be so tough, stay away from me. There is nothing between us now.'' She shook her head for emphasis. ''Nothing.''

Hunter drew in a deep breath, moving a fraction away from her. ''That's where you're wrong. There's everything between us. History. Hurt. Sex. I look at you and remember everything we shared.''

Aimee swore softly. He was right. There was too much between them for indifference. It would be a battle to stay away from him. A battle she would win if it killed her.

"Fine," she said stiffly. "Remember all you want, just keep it to yourself."

Turning, she pushed through the screen door and stepped out into the night. The darkness enfolded her, comforting in its blackness. She hurried into the yard and toward her house, fighting the urge to run. The urge to look back.

Hunter watched her. She felt his gaze upon her as an almost palpable thing, compelling her to come back to him. Heat stung her cheeks, and she shook her head, scolding herself, her imagination. And her weakness when it came to Hunter.

Hadn't the past taught her anything?

Of course it had, she assured herself. Hunter had been right, there was so much between them, so much history, it would be difficult at first to keep from being swept away by those potent memories. After all, wouldn't every ex-couple experience the same?

Aimee slowed her steps. But had they ever been a couple, in the traditional sense of the word? They'd been together. They'd been intimate. But had he ever felt a part of her or as if she belonged to him?

She thought not. And that hurt. Still. After everything she'd been through and after all the time that had passed. It shouldn't hurt; she didn't want it to.

She reached the house and climbed the steps to the gallery. She paused then and looked back, knowing Hunter could no longer see her. He stood in the doorway still, a strong, dark silhouette against the rectangle of light. Always an island. Always alone.

From behind her came the gravelly cry of an egret as it roosted in a live oak at the water's edge. The bayou lapped against the shore; a nutria or some other small animal scurried from the brush into the cool, dark water. Time inched past. Hunter didn't move.

Aimee drew her eyebrows together, feeling his loneliness, his self-imposed exile as she always had—deeply and in a place with an infinite capacity for love. And hope.

And for self-delusion.

She shook her head and turned away from him. Crossing the gallery, she let herself into the house. Empathy for Hunter had brought her nothing but heartache. Believing she could change his life, believing he would love her had hurt even more.

She was done with believing and hoping and deluding. She was a grown-up now; she would do what was best for her and Oliver, no matter the personal toll.

Aimee flipped off the lights, then went to check on Oliver. He sprawled across his small bed, his covers a tangle at his feet. Smiling tenderly, Aimee reached down and stroked the soft, silky curls at his nape. He was losing those baby curls already. His big-boy hair was coming in more like hers, thick, straight and heavy.

Bending down, she pressed a light kiss on his temple. He stirred and whimpered. She'd meant what she'd said to Hunter—she loved Oliver more than anything. She would go through hell and beyond for him.

How could she regret having met Hunter?

Aimee drew the quilt over Oliver, tucking it snugly around him, thinking of the way Hunter had gone blank after she'd spoken of her love for Oliver. As if he'd retreated to a place where neither she nor anybody else could touch him.

She'd recognized the expression. When they'd been together, every so often he would zone out. And afterward he had always been quieter, more remote, than usual.

She'd always suspected he'd been thinking of his wife and son and had tried to coax him into talking to her. Into sharing his thoughts and feelings. He never had. That he'd never been able to talk to her, to share his pain, had hurt her deeply.

She shook her head. But then, that had always been the problem between them. She'd shared everything, given everything. And he'd been willing to give her nothing—of himself, of his heart.

Tears filled her eyes and she blinked against them. Well, she wouldn't share Oliver. And she wouldn't worry about Hunter's problems. His needs. She had her own to deal with.

Taking one last look at her son, Aimee headed to her own bedroom. She stepped out of her shorts and T-shirt and into a light cotton nightgown. As if drawn by a force beyond her control, her gaze strayed to the window. She gazed at the dark rectangle a moment, then unable to stop herself, crossed to it and looked out. She sucked in a sharp breath—Hunter still stood in the doorway.

Aimee stared at him, her mouth dry, her heart fast. The urge to slip out of the house and go to him moved over her, so strong she shook with the effort of holding back.

A fool. She was a fool. He didn't want her. He'd made that plain, back then and now. Curling her fingers into her palms, Aimee turned resolutely away from the window. She wouldn't give in to her feelings, she vowed, crossing to her cold bed. Not this time, no matter the price.

"Good morning."

Aimee looked up from the toast she was buttering. Hunter stood in the doorway, his hair damp from his shower, his eyes still heavy lidded and sexy with sleep. He rubbed his knuckles across his jaw, smooth from his morning shave, and she caught herself following the movement of his hand and swore silently. She'd always liked watching him shave. For her, there had been something erotic about the totally masculine act.

She met his gaze then and he smiled, the curving of his lips slow and supremely male. She gritted her teeth. She would not allow herself to be affected by him. She simply would not.

"Morning," she said, knowing she sounded ungracious but not giving a damn.

"Sleep well?"

"Fine," she lied. She'd tossed and turned, her head filled with Hunter, the past and present colliding in her dreams. When, just after first light, she'd dragged herself out of bed, she'd half expected to look out the window and find him still standing in his doorway.

Of course, he hadn't been.

"Am I too early?" he asked, shooting her another cocky smile.

Aimee resumed buttering the toast, annoyed. He knew he wasn't. Oliver sat in his booster chair, stuffing grapes in his mouth as fast as he could, Roubin sat at the table with the fisherman's almanac and a big earthenware mug of coffee.

"Of course not," she muttered. "Coffee's on the stove, cups are in the cabinet beside the refrigerator."

"Thanks." He sauntered into the kitchen, heading for the coffeepot.

Oliver eyed Hunter warily as he poured his coffee. "Maman," he asked around a grape, "why here?"

Aimee smiled reassuringly at her son and placed the plate of toast on the table. She had prepared for this moment. "Mr. Hunter is renting the room behind the store." She quartered a slice of toast and set it in front of him. "He's decided to stay and visit."

Oliver frowned, looking from his mother to Hunter and back. "Why?"

"Why?" Aimee repeated, surprised. Oliver usually accepted her word without question. "Well, he...he's never been to Louisiana before, and he's going to do some sightseeing. Doesn't that sound fun?" She smiled. "Now, eat your toast."

Again, Oliver looked questioningly from his mother to Hunter, then frowned and dropped his gaze to his plate.

Roubin peered over the top of his almanac; Hunter cleared his throat, and Aimee let out a frustrated breath. Off to a great start, she thought, starting on the eggs. Even her three-year-old son knew something was up.

Hunter carried his coffee to the table, choosing the chair on Oliver's right. He started to sit down and the boy jerked his head up. "No! Maman's!"

Hunter blinked in surprise, then smiled and took the other empty chair. "Sorry about that, Bud..."

Aimee looked at Hunter. His expression was frozen with pain. *Buddy.* That was what he used to call Pete. She only knew because his sister had let it slip once when they had all been together. She'd been stunned to learn that Aimee hadn't known that. When Aimee had confronted Hunter with it later, he'd been angry that his sister had brought it up.

Her chest aching with the memory, Aimee quickly finished scrambling the eggs. "Here we go," she said with forced brightness. She crossed to the table and spooned some eggs onto each plate. After she served Hunter, she lightly touched his shoulder. "Is that enough?"

He met her gaze and she saw by his blank look that he was a million miles away and had no idea what she was talking about. A second later his eyes cleared, he looked down at his plate, then back up at her. "Yes," he murmured. "Thank you."

He looked away, a mask of indifference slipping over his expression once more. He was shutting her out. She felt the door slam between them as keenly as if it had been a real door, solid and unbreakable.

Hunter remained silent through the rest of the meal. He avoided her gaze and he never again looked at Oliver. Not really, anyway. As if drawn to the child, he would glance his way, then as if catching himself doing so, would quickly avert his gaze. When Oliver talked or laughed, Hunter shifted in his seat, stiffening almost imperceptibly.

Through the meal Roubin, too, remained noticeably quiet. Aimee was uncertain whether her father was studying Hunter or judging her. Or both. She only knew that his silent perusal made her jumpy.

Finally, when she began to clear the table, he spoke up. "What time is my appointment with that *imposteur?*"

Aimee frowned at her father. "Dr. Landry is expecting to see you at two."

He gestured with his big right hand. "Cancel. We have no one to watch the store."

Aimee wiped Oliver's face. "Ti-tante Marie is coming. She will sit for Oliver also. She's looking forward to it."

Roubin snorted with disgust. "Marie, she is so clumsy. Every time she comes, *voilà!* Things are broken. It is no good to have her alone in the store."

"That's only happened a few times, Papa." Aimee wiped Oliver's sticky hands. "And you know how much Oliver likes her. Everything will be fine."

He scowled. "What of the lures, eh? Can Marie get that mess untangled?"

Aimee made a sound of frustration and tossed the washcloth in the sink. "The lures have waited this long to be untangled, they can wait a bit longer. This appointment has been set up for three months, Papa. You *are* going to see Dr. Landry today."

Roubin grunted and muttered something uncomplimentary about doctors and daughters. She opened her mouth to reply but Oliver tugged on her arm, stopping her. She looked down at her son.

"Swing, Maman?"

"Sure, baby. I'll get cousin Alphonse to fix it."

"Now?" he asked, his expression hopeful.

"I'll call him today." She smiled and kissed Oliver's head. "Go on now and play in your room."

Oliver scooted off his booster seat and raced out of the kitchen. She watched him go, then turned back to her father. "Papa, I'm sorry. But you know this is for your own good."

He shook his head. "I know that if you were truly sorry, *chère,* you would not make me go." Roubin pushed his wheelchair away from the table, slowly and as with great effort. He sighed. "My own daughter, she has turned against me."

"That's not true!" Aimee cried, angling a glance at Hunter, uncomfortable with his presence. He faced the other way, his attention on the *Acadiana Times* and his coffee. She suspected instead that he was soaking in every word of her and her father's exchange.

She looked once again at her father. The defeated line of his shoulders, the bitter set of his mouth, tugged at her heartstrings. "Dr. Landry needs to check to make sure your condition hasn't changed. It's a precaution."

Roubin's lips twisted and he lifted his hands, palms up. "Look at me, *chère.* Has anything changed? I'm still an invalid, *non?* Still useless."

Tears filled her eyes, and she crossed to him. Bending down, she pressed her cheek to his. "You're not useless, Papa. You're still the head of this family. We depend on you."

He snorted with disgust. "How can a man be the head of his family when he is unable even to make a decision about his own body? I'm not sick, yet you insist on taking me to see the *traître.*" He shook his head. "*Non,* my life, she is over."

The newspaper crackled, and Aimee slid another glance at Hunter, this one withering. If he possessed an ounce of compassion or sensitivity, he would excuse himself. Annoyed, she stood and positioned herself behind her father's chair. Well, if he wouldn't leave, she would.

"It's time to open up, Papa. I'll wheel you over."

But she thought, narrowing her eyes, she wasn't about to let Hunter get off so easily. They *would* discuss this later.

"Oliver," she called, "I'm wheeling your *pépère* to the store. I'll be right back."

Fifteen minutes later Aimee stalked back into the kitchen. Hunter still sat at the table, reading the paper. She quickly checked on Oliver, then returned to face Hunter.

She stopped in front of him, drawing in an angry breath when he didn't acknowledge her in any way. "How dare you eavesdrop on my conversation with my father?"

Hunter looked up at her. He lifted his eyebrows coolly. "If you were worried about my overhearing your conversation, perhaps you should have had it elsewhere. I was just sitting here minding my own business."

"I doubt that." She rested her fists on her hips. "Besides, if you had any manners, or sensitivity for that matter, you would have excused yourself. After all, my father is bound to a wheelchair. He can't just pop up and walk out like you can."

"That's what he'd like you to believe."

She narrowed her eyes. "Excuse me? Are you saying my father can walk?"

"Of course not." Hunter folded the paper, then tossed it on the table. "I'm talking about his pitiful woe-is-me act."

Heat flew to her cheeks. "Great bedside manner, Doc. Really sensitive." Furious, Aimee swung away from him. She crossed to the sink and began to fill it.

"And he has you falling for it hook, line and sinker." Hunter stood and crossed to her. "Your father is manipulating you, Aimee."

She met his gaze. "That's not true."

"He's using your feelings for him to get his way. Your guilt. Your frustration and love."

"And that's absolutely untrue." She shut off the water and with jerky movements began to wash the dishes. "I resent you saying it."

"Do you?"

"Yes!"

He lifted one corner of his mouth in a lopsided smile. "You didn't give in to him?"

"Give in to him?" She lifted her chin. "I don't know what you're talking about."

He leaned toward her, trapping her gaze. "Did you cancel his doctor appointment, Aimee? That's what he wanted. It's what that whole conversation was about."

A glass slipped from her hands and into the soapy water. She heard it crack on the bottom of the sink. "I thought you were minding your own business?"

"You gave in then, didn't you?"

The heat in her cheeks became fire, and she swore silently. She didn't have to explain anything to Hunter Powell. He was neither a friend nor a family member, nor was he her father's doctor. It infuriated her that she felt the need to anyway.

She shot him a withering glance, then turned back to her dishes. "I agreed to cancel the appointment. But not because he manipulated me into it. He's in pain. He feels his life, his entire reason for living, has been taken away from him. And he was right, it is *his* body."

At the look in Hunter's eyes, guilt curled through her. She told herself she had nothing to feel guilty over, that she'd done the right thing. She buried her hands in the soapy water. "What's wrong with letting him have some dignity? How you can stand there and judge us when you're not in our—"

Aimee cried out and pulled her hands from the water. A long gash marred the side of her right hand and blood ran down her arm and into the pillows of white suds. She stared blankly at the growing circle of red.

"God, Aimee." Hunter grabbed the dish towel she had taken from a drawer only moments ago. He pressed it firmly against the cut. "Sit down." When she didn't move he led her to a chair, still holding the towel in place. "You're white as a sheet. Put your head between your knees."

"I'm fine. Really, I'm not going to fain..." She moaned as her senses began to swim. Feeling like a total idiot, she lowered her head to her knees and began sucking in deep, steadying breaths.

As her head cleared she became aware of Hunter—the warmth of his body pressed close to hers, the low, comforting sound of his voice against her ear, the feel of his hand in her hair, softly stroking. He meant to comfort and calm. Not to arouse, not to seduce.

Even as she told herself that, tongues of fire began to lick at her. She groaned and called herself a fool.

"Aimee? Are you okay?"

"Yes," she whispered, lifting her head.

"You've got some color back," he murmured thickly, not taking his hand from her hair.

She couldn't quite meet his eyes. "It's total embarrassment. I feel like a big baby."

"Don't." He ran his fingers through her hair. "You had a shock."

She told herself to inch away from his touch, to ask him to stop, to tell him she could take care of herself. She didn't move a muscle. "It's just a little cut."

"That remains to be seen." He searched her gaze. "Feel steady enough for me to take a look?"

Steady? With him so close? What a laugh. She nodded. "Go for it."

Hunter let up on the towel, easing it carefully from the cut. She turned her head away, squeezing her eyes shut, her head beginning to swim again. "How bad?"

"Hmm."

He poked gently at it and she winced. "What does 'hmm' mean?"

"That it could be a lot worse."

She swallowed hard. "Do I need . . . stitches?"

He laughed and touched the tip of her nose with his index finger. "Nope. I think once we get it cleaned up and bandaged you'll be okay. Which way to the first-aid kit?"

Aimee led him to the bathroom, then sat on the commode while he got out the antiseptic and bandages. He squatted down in front of her, then met her eyes. "This is going to sting."

She sucked in a sharp breath as he applied the antiseptic. "I can't believe I forgot about that glass," she said, uncomfortably looking away. "Dumb."

"It happens."

He finished cleaning the wound, then bandaged it. Aimee watched him work, gazing down at the top of his golden head, studying his hands as they moved on her skin. He had the best hands—long and strong, with blunt-tipped fingers. She'd always thought them sexy. A doctor's hands. Or an artist's.

Or a lover's.

Memories of other times those hands had been on her body filled her head. Times they had pleasured, times they had stolen both her breath and her sanity. Heat began to lick at her again, heat that had nothing to do with her cut and everything to do with Hunter.

She sucked in a sharp breath and he glanced up. "Are you okay?"

She nodded, her mouth dry. "Fine."

He returned his gaze to his work. "You always did have an aversion to the sight of blood. Remember the time you stepped on that piece of glass in the park?"

"You had to carry me back to the car," she managed, her voice thick.

"Mmm." He rubbed his fingers softly, rhythmically across the bandage. A smile pulled at the corners of his mouth. "Some hero. It practically killed me."

"It was almost a mile."

"Almost two." He looked up again. Their eyes met. And held. "Do you remember how you thanked me?"

Her heart stopped, then started again with a vengeance. The breath shuddered past her lips. "Yes," she whispered, lowering her head. "I remember."

He tangled his fingers in her hair and tugged gently. Her head lowered more; her eyelids fluttered shut. She parted her lips.

"Maman! Where are you?"

Aimee jerked her head up, stunned. Dear Lord, what had she been thinking of? She'd been about to kiss him. If Oliver hadn't interrupted, she would have.

Fighting for breath, she sneaked a glance at Hunter. She saw her own feelings mirrored in his eyes—relief, disappointment. Unrelieved desire.

She folded her shaking hands in her lap. "I'm here, baby. In the bathroom."

Oliver raced into the room, stopping abruptly in front of them. He looked from one to the other, then he saw her bandage. His baby face filled with concern. "Owie?"

"Yes." She smiled tremulously. "Bad owie."

"Kiss make better?" he asked.

Aimee found Hunter's gaze, arousal tightening in her gut. *Kiss make better.* She'd wanted his mouth on hers so badly it hurt. It still did.

Aimee looked away, her cheeks hot. Why was she so weak when it came to this man?

"Maman?"

Aimee looked at her son once more and nodded. Oliver bent and kissed the bandage, then solemnly met her eyes. "All better."

"All better," she repeated, lifting her gaze to Hunter's. But he'd already retreated from her. In his expression she saw nothing of the moment they had just shared, nothing of the longing, the memories.

Hurt, she straightened her shoulders and eased her hand from his grasp. Again, she said a silent thanks that Oliver had shown up when he had.

"That ought to do it," Hunter said stiffly and stood. "I suggest a couple of aspirin and a nap. If you have any problems, give me a . . . I'll be around."

And then he turned and walked away. Aimee watched him go, the strangest sensation in the pit of her stomach—a combination of sadness, relief and hurt. Telling herself it was for the best, she turned her attention back to her son.

Chapter Four

As the days passed, Hunter couldn't forget those electric moments between him and Aimee. They'd shaken him, shaken his faith in his ability to remain emotionally distant from her. Shaken his belief in his ability to simply do the right thing by her and Oliver and move on.

Hunter leaned his head against the rocking chair's high back and gazed up at the crazily spinning ceiling fan. He'd almost kissed her. She'd almost let him. They'd both known better; neither wanted an involvement with the other.

He shifted his gaze. A handful of tourists, eager for mementos of their visit to the Louisiana bayou, had been milling around the store for twenty minutes now, Aimee helping them. Hunter smiled as he heard her speak—she laid the patois on pretty thick for the tourists. Not to try to sell more of the crafts and trinkets Roubin hated so much, but because the customers enjoyed it.

Aimee liked people; she always had. And people had always responded to her. Watching her now with the tourists, she reminded him more of the woman he had known three and a half years ago. The woman who had wowed and charmed everyone she met. Including him.

As she directed a customer to another part of the store, Aimee caught him watching her. Their eyes met, then she turned quickly away. Hunter wasn't surprised. Ever since their near kiss, Aimee had given him a wide berth, keeping a room's distance between them—at least—all the time. She'd not spoken directly to him, nor had she met his eyes. But he'd felt her gaze upon him when she thought his attention was elsewhere. He'd felt her tension, her turbulent emotions. Her annoyance at his constant presence.

Oliver seemed to have taken his cue from Aimee. He kept his distance; he, too, studied Hunter when he thought Hunter was unaware. He'd sensed Oliver didn't quite trust him, whether because the boy had picked up on his mother's feelings or Hunter's own mixed emotions Hunter wasn't certain.

But whichever, Oliver's wariness suited Hunter perfectly. The last thing he wanted was Oliver's interest or attention. He hadn't taken up residence in La Fin to be drawn into Oliver's life, only to fulfill his fiscal responsibility to him.

Besides, Hunter was accustomed to hanging back, to separating himself and observing. He preferred it that way.

Hunter frowned down at the technothriller he held in his hands, at the paragraph he'd reread three times in the same number of minutes. The truth was, he was already too involved. He found himself thinking about Roubin, Aimee and their relationship, found himself thinking about Roubin's illness. He'd even toyed with the idea of contacting Roubin's doctor himself, before reminding himself to butt out.

His frown deepened. Just being around Aimee had been difficult. Since the incident with the broken glass, damn near impossible, really. He looked at her and remembered touching her, making love to her. He remembered what it had been like to bask in her smile, her warmth. He found himself wanting to reach out a hand to stroke, found himself feeling possessive of her, as if it were his right.

It wasn't his right, he reminded himself. He had nothing to offer her; he had hurt her. He would hurt her again if he gave in to his need to touch her.

During the day, those reminders had kept things in perspective. Nothing helped vision like the harsh light of day. But at night, alone in the heat, the only breeze the one stirred by the ceiling fan above his bed, reminders weren't worth dip. Impulse came with the dark; passion overrode sense during those still, sultry hours.

So, night after night he lay alone in his bed, remembering, longing for her, battling the ache in his loins and the urge to cross the lawn and make her his once again.

Giving up all pretense of reading, Hunter made a sound of disgust and shut the book. Even more potent, he admitted, more painful, were the memories conjured by being around Oliver.

He lifted his gaze. Aimee stood directly across from him, talking with a customer. She held Oliver in her arms; he snuggled against her, his arms wrapped around her neck, his legs her middle. The boy's eyes drooped sleepily and Aimee rocked gently back and forth as she talked.

It hurt to watch them. Flat out. On a gut level, the place where he had *felt* being a parent, in the place that had once welled with pride and tenderness while watching Ginny hold Pete the very same way.

Hunter fisted his fingers against the pain. As he watched, Aimee lightly stroked Oliver's hair; every so often she would touch his cheek or the back of his neck. The gestures were ones of love, of ownership, ones that strengthened the physical bond between parent and child.

He'd touched Pete the same way. A lifetime ago. Then it had seemed as natural as breathing—now it seemed strange, foreign. The man he'd been five years ago was a world away from the one he was today. Hunter drew his eyebrows together and shifted uncomfortably in the rocking chair. Was he even capable of such tenderness, such love, any more?

He thought not. That part of him had died with Ginny and Pete.

Although looking at Oliver and knowing he was a part of the child but not a part of his life tugged strangely at him. It felt odd, knowing he was connected to Oliver in the most basic way, without ever having touched him at all—certainly not in the small, possessive ways of a parent. Odd, knowing that in all probability he never would.

He'd missed that part of being a parent. He hadn't realized how much until this moment. The memory of how Pete's skin had felt, baby smooth and as soft as rose petals, slipped out of his strongbox of memories and filled his head. Hunter's throat closed with emotion. Pete had liked his back rubbed as he drifted off to sleep. Hunter remembered continuing to stroke him long after Pete fell asleep, just because it felt so good to touch him.

Hunter squeezed his eyes shut, fighting the sweet memory because he knew what would follow it, fighting even though he knew it was too late. With his mind's eye he saw Pete, angelic in sleep, curled up on his side, his favorite toy, Toby Tiger, clutched to him. Hunter felt his mouth lifting at the mental picture, the joy of it filling him. Although a towhead, Pete had had long, dark eyelashes. Women had laughed about how unfair it was for a boy to have such lashes. In sleep they had formed soft, dark crescents against his downy cheeks, and his rose-colored mouth had been pouty in total relaxation.

Suddenly, the image in his head shifted, changing into another image, that of the very last time he'd seen his baby. Not sleeping. Not angelic though surely with the angels then.

Pain, swift and sharp, knifed through him. Jumping to his feet, Hunter strode out to the gallery, directly into the harsh sun. His eyes teared, then ran. He sucked in a deep breath, hoping to clear his head, but instead filling it with the smell of the morgue. And of the fire.

"I'm sorry, Mr. Powell, but I have to do this. Is this your son?"

Hunter's stomach pitched, the bile rising in his throat, hysteria with it.

His baby. His little Pete.

Hunter pressed the heels of his hands to his eyes, the nightmare upon him.

"And this? Is this your wife?"

Dear God. Ginny . . . Ginny . . .

He'd lost it then, crumbling. They'd had to drag him out; he hadn't wanted to leave them there like that. They deserved so much better. His boy. His wife. In that moment he had understood the madness that sometimes takes a person at the death of a loved one.

"Why not me instead?" he'd cried. *"Why not me instead?"*

The screen door squeaked, and Hunter opened his eyes. Oliver peeked at him from around the door, his dark gaze unblinking and full of curiosity.

Hunter stared at the child, the terror retreating, reality and a sense of equilibrium returning. He put a hand on the cypress column for support and tried to smile. He failed miserably.

For a moment it looked as if Oliver was going to duck back inside without speaking, then he pursed his lips thoughtfully. "Owie?" he asked.

Hunter made a choked sound and nodded. Oliver cocked his head, moving his gaze over Hunter. He frowned. "Where it hurt?"

Emotion rose in Hunter's throat and he flexed his fingers, forcing the emotion back, fighting for control. "Here," he said finally, thickly, pressing a hand to his chest, to his heart.

Oliver was silent for a moment as if considering that. Then he inched the rest of the way through the door and crossed hesitantly to Hunter, stopping in front of him.

The boy tipped his head back to look up at Hunter. "Kiss make better?"

Hunter's breath caught. Pete had started doing that, right before he . . . before the end. He had started pressing soft, sloppy kisses on every hurt, real or imaginary.

Hunter shook his head, a thread of panic curling through him, recoiling at the idea of a child other than Pete kissing him. "I don't think so," he murmured, taking a step back. "Thanks, but I . . . don't . . . need . . ."

Hunter's words faltered as he gazed down at Oliver's face. In it he saw trust and the simple, unshakable belief that a kiss really had the ability to take pain away. Oliver didn't know him; judging by his previous behavior, he didn't even quite trust him. Yet, he was offering to take his pain away. Hunter swallowed past the knot of emotion in his throat. Oliver was offering him a gift born out of pure love for a fellow human being.

Nothing could be less—or more—complicated.

He couldn't turn Oliver down, Hunter thought gazing at the little boy's upturned face. Oliver wouldn't understand the refusal. He didn't yet have the ability, hadn't yet experienced enough of life's hard knocks.

But if he had the ability, he never would have made the offer.

That meant something, Hunter realized. It was important. And suddenly, more than anything in the world, he wanted the gift of healing this child offered.

Hunter dropped to Oliver's level. The boy looked into his eyes for one brief moment, then leaned forward and touched his lips to the place directly over Hunter's heart.

As light as the stroke of a butterfly's wing, Oliver's touch hit Hunter with the force of a punch to the gut. Hunter sucked in a sharp breath, the aftershocks ricocheting through him.

"Oliver?"

Hunter shifted his gaze to the doorway. Aimee stood there, her expression blank with surprise. She opened her mouth to speak, then shut it.

Oliver turned and ran to his mother. He paused when he reached her, taking a quick peek back at Hunter. A ghost of a smile touched his mouth, then he ducked into the store. Without saying a word, Aimee followed him.

Hunter stared at the empty doorway for long moments, his thoughts a jumble.

Kiss make better.

Hunter shook his head, the strangest sensation building inside him. A sensation at once heavy and light, brilliant and dark. An ache. A sweetness.

A need.

Hunter shook his head in denial. He was becoming fanciful. He'd been moved by the child's generosity, by the darkness of his own memories. That was all.

He needed to get away from Aimee and Oliver, this place. He needed a couple of hours' change of scenery, needed something to occupy his mind other than the past and the dynamics of a family he had no business becoming involved with.

He had to find a way to put more emotional distance between himself, Aimee and Oliver.

Straightening, Hunter crossed the gallery and descended the stairs to his car. As he opened the door, he looked back at the store. Aimee stood at the window. Something in her expression pulled at him and for long moments, he stood unmoving, his gaze locked with hers. Then he broke the contact, climbed into his car and drove away.

It took Hunter nearly three hours to put what had occurred between him and Oliver into perspective, and to rationalize how the boy's gesture had made him feel. During that time he'd also assured himself that he was not becoming involved in Aimee or Oliver's life. He'd reasoned that he hadn't totally recovered from the shock of discovering he had another child. Once he did, he wouldn't have any problem maintaining his emotional distance.

Sure.

Hunter parked his car beside the store and stepped out into the early afternoon sun. An older woman sat in a rocking chair on the gallery, Oliver asleep in her lap. She looked up and smiled as he approached.

"You must be Hunter," she said in a voice heavily laced with the Cajun patois. "I'm Marie. Roubin's sister."

Her smile was broad, genuine and full of warmth. Hunter found himself returning it in kind. "It's a pleasure to meet you."

She looked him over, her expression openly curious. He wondered if she'd been told of his relationship to Oliver. If she had, he saw no antagonism in her expression, no judgment.

"You are a friend of Aimee's from California."

It wasn't a question, but he answered anyway. "Yes."

"Me, I've never been to California." She laughed. "But I've been to Shreveport."

Hunter stopped at the base of the stairs. "Well, you have me there. I've never been to Shreveport."

"You are not missing much."

Hunter laughed, liking Marie's sense of humor. Her openness. "Is Aimee here?"

"*Non*. She took Roubin to New Orleans. To see the physical therapist." She clucked her tongue. "What a mess! My brother, he is not a good patient."

"I've noticed," Hunter murmured, unwittingly shifting his gaze from hers to the sleeping Oliver.

"He is beautiful, *non?*"

Hunter looked up at the woman, then back at Oliver, a catch in his chest. "He looks like his mother."

"More than you know, *cher*. I could show you photographs." She shook her head and clucked her tongue again. "*Incroyable!* They are like mirror images."

Hunter told himself to murmur a nicety or two, then excuse himself. Instead, he found himself climbing the stairs. "Really?"

"Of course, there are differences. He is a boy, after all. But he looks like Roubin, too. And like me." Marie threaded her fingers through Oliver's hair. "The Boudreaux blood, it is strong. No matter who we marry, our babies, they look like our people."

She shook her head and squinted at a car that drove past, then lifted her hand in greeting. Turning back to him, she looked him straight in the eye. "Your blood, it is good?"

Hunter met her gaze just as seriously as she met his. "I like to think so."

For a moment she remained silent as she rocked the chair rhythmically back and forth, then she angled him a glance from the corners of her eyes. "You are enjoying your visit?"

"Very much."

"The bayou, she is beautiful. *Non?*"

"Yes."

The chair creaked as Marie shifted her weight. "And so are her women. The most beautiful in the world. You agree?"

She gave him a look that dared him to disagree. Hunter smiled. But how could he? He'd always thought Aimee the most beautiful woman he'd ever known. "I do agree. Present company included."

Marie colored with pleasure. "And Aimee, she has been cooking for you?" When he nodded, she continued, "She is a good cook. She makes the gumbo, the *étouffée*, the couscous. She has cooked these for you?"

Marie was matchmaking, Hunter realized. Gently. But with about as much subtlety as a steamroller. Instead of making him uncomfortable, Marie's obvious love and concern for Aimee pleased him. He fought a smile, imagining what Aimee's reaction to this conversation would be if she could somehow overhear it. She would be furious.

Hunter settled into the rocker next to hers. "Some," he answered.

"*Bon.*"

The woman said the word as if Hunter's fate was now sealed. Little did she know, Hunter thought ruefully, that Aimee wouldn't have him even if he had the ability to make a commitment.

"Poor Aimee," Marie murmured. "My brother, he is so stubborn. He makes it very difficult for her to be a good daughter." The woman sighed. "It has always been hard between them. They are so different, yet so much the same. If there had been other children, maybe things would have been otherwise. But Roubin and his Rose were only blessed with Aimee. It was a great tragedy for them." She readjusted Oliver in her lap, and the small boy whimpered in protest. "My brother, he pinned so many hopes on Aimee, that when she wanted to leave...well, they fought bitterly over it."

Aimee hadn't talked much about her family, not in terms of problems anyway. Not in terms of dynamics. She'd described them all, had talked lovingly of both her people and the bayou. Although she'd mentioned his stubbornness, she had spoken only with pride of her father.

And sadness, Hunter remembered, frowning. Aimee had always sounded sad when speaking of her father and her home. She'd written letters to her father, but to Hunter's knowledge, she had never received any in return.

Let it drop, he told himself. This definitely qualified in the "getting too involved, maintain distance" category. Instead, he turned back to Marie. "What happened?"

She shrugged. "My brother, he thought he could keep her with him through guilt. And shame. But he could not. It broke his heart when she left, yet still he closed the door."

Hunter reached out to touch Oliver's silky hair, then realizing what he was doing, frowned and dropped his hand. "What do you mean, closed the door?"

"He told her she was dead to him, to the family, until she came back to her people. Until she was ready to be a good daughter, to do her duty toward him." At Hunter's shocked expression, she said, "You did not know any of this?"

When Hunter shook his head, she continued, "It was very bad. Both so unhappy. But both so stubborn." She lifted her shoulders. "Even when Roubin became ill, he would not relent. He forbade any of us to contact her. It caused us all great pain, but we felt we must respect his wishes."

Her father had suffered his aneurysm while she was gone. Aimee had come home to a father she barely recognized.

Hunter's heart went out to her. He could imagine how much that had hurt. How guilty she must have felt.

Inside the phone jangled. Oliver whimpered, then stirred. Without warning, Marie stood and placed the child in Hunter's lap. *"Pardon, cher.* I will be right back."

Hunter watched her go, adrenaline pumping through him. As the screen door slapped shut, he looked down at Oliver. The boy whimpered again and snuggled against his chest, nestling his head into the curve of his arm.

Hunter swallowed. What the hell did he do now?

He looked anxiously back at the door; from inside he could hear Marie's deep voice as she spoke to whoever had called. Hunter looked back down at Oliver, emotion knotting in his chest, making it difficult to breathe. The boy was warm with sleep, so warm his hair and T-shirt were damp with sweat. So warm, the heat seemed to be pouring out of Oliver and into him. The warmth spread, filling him. His tensed muscles eased, then liquefied, and he relaxed back against the rocker.

Hunter breathed deeply through his nose, drawing in Oliver's scent, one that was both sweet and sweaty. Pete used to smell the same way, he remembered. Especially in the summer, or after an hour of particularly strenuous play.

A lump in his throat, Hunter lightly touched Oliver's hair, brushing the damp curls from where they clung to his neck. He squeezed his eyes shut. Dear God, it felt good to hold Oliver in his arms like this. The way he used to hold Pete.

The screen door opened and Marie stepped through, carrying a pitcher of lemonade and three glasses. "That was Roberto," she said. "For Aimee."

Hunter looked blankly at Marie.

"He is in love with her," Marie explained. "He is Cajun, but his blood, it is not so good." She slid her gaze coyly to Hunter's. "But who knows? Our Aimee, she will do what she wants. And Oliver, he needs a father."

Hunter frowned, denying that the feeling moving over him was jealousy. "This . . . Roberto, he's in love with Aimee?"

"*Oui.*" Marie poured the lemonade and handed him a glass. "And he is a determined man. A man who goes after what he wants."

And he wanted Aimee, Hunter thought. His Aimee.

As the thought passed through his head, Hunter reminded himself that Aimee was not *his*. He also told himself that he didn't care in the least that Aimee was involved with some guy named Roberto. He was glad Aimee had begun a new life. He wanted her to be happy. Sure.

Then why did he suddenly feel like flattening some guy he'd never even met before?

Fighting off both the thought and the urge, he took a sip of the lemonade. Working to keep his tone casual, he asked, "She and this...Roberto are seeing each other?"

Marie hesitated. "They see each other. Yes."

He tightened his fingers on the glass. "It sounds serious."

"This bothers you?"

"Of course not," Hunter said quickly, his voice sounding gruff to his own ears. "It's none of my business. None at all," he repeated firmly, moving the chair in a gentle rocking motion.

Marie watched him for a moment, then smiled. "It is something we never forget, *non?* How to love a child."

Hunter looked down at Oliver, realizing with a shock how he'd been rocking him. How he'd been cradling him in his arms as if he belonged there. As if Oliver were his.

"I love you, Daddy."

"I love you, too, Buddy. Forever and ever."

Guilt curled through him, squeezing, choking. Hunter set aside his glass, stood and handed Oliver back to Marie. She took the boy, the expression in her eyes quizzical.

"I don't want him to awake in my arms and be frightened," Hunter murmured, his voice thick. He took a step back. "It was nice meeting you, Marie. I'm sure we'll see each other again before I leave." He took another step. "If you'll excuse me, I've got some things to take care of."

"Certainement." Marie stood, Oliver nestled in her arms. "But before you go, could you do for me a favor?"

Hunter hesitated, his gaze going to Oliver once again. "Sure."

Marie led him into the store. "Alphonse called earlier. He's going to bring some shrimp tomorrow. To sell in the store. I went to clean the scale, and she slipped from her hook. It's too heavy for me or Aimee, and Roubin... he gets so frustrated when he can't do for himself."

Hunter eyed the scale and its chains, set in a neat heap on the counter, then the hook in the ceiling above. "No problem. Is there a ladder?"

"*Oui*. In back."

Hunter retrieved the ladder, and set it up. As he picked up the heavy old contraption, Oliver stirred, then yawned. "Maman," he murmured, his eyes still tight shut.

"*Non, bébé. Ti-tante.*"

Oliver opened his eyes and smiled sleepily up at his great-aunt. "Maman coming home soon?"

"*Oui.*"

He shifted his gaze to Hunter, then hid his face in his aunt's blouse. "What he doing?"

"Rehanging the scale. Cousin Alphonse is bringing some shrimp tomorrow. Maybe your *maman*, she will make some bisque."

Oliver peeked back at Hunter, studying him intently, watching as he effortlessly rehung the unwieldy old scale.

"There," Hunter said, descending the ladder, being careful to keep his gaze from straying to Oliver. "Anything else while I have the ladder out?"

"Swing." Oliver squirmed in Marie's arms, and she set him down. Wordlessly, he crossed to Hunter and slipped his small hand into Hunter's large one. Hunter stared at their joined hands, his mouth dry, his heart fast.

Oliver tugged. "Swing."

Swallowing hard, Hunter let the boy lead him through the back of the store and out onto the back porch. Oliver pointed to the oak tree and the swing hanging dejectedly by one rope.

Oliver looked up at Hunter, his expression at once grim and hopeful. "You fix it?"

Hunter looked at the broken swing, then back down at Oliver's face, a warm sensation moving over him. Hunter smiled and squeezed Oliver's hand. "You got it . . . Tiger. I'll get the ladder."

Chapter Five

Aimee and Roubin arrived home as the sky shifted from the blue of afternoon to the lavender of evening. Aimee helped her father from the car and into his chair, then pushed him up the ramp. Exhaustion pulled at her, as did a heart-deep weariness brought on by her father's predicament and her place in it.

The trip had been a disaster. Her father had been difficult—short-tempered and uncooperative. He'd taken his bitterness and anger out on her. It seemed the more accommodating she had become, the worse he'd treated her.

Several times during the course of the afternoon she'd had to fight off tears. It hurt to have him treat her so. It hurt more to see him so unhappy. She had made it through the day by reminding herself that her father needed her, that she was being a good, dutiful daughter, just as she'd promised herself she would be.

"Oliver," Aimee called, holding the screen open with one hand and helping to guide Roubin's chair through the store's doorway with the other. "We're home."

The screen snapped shut behind them, the sound echoing in the empty store. Aimee frowned. She had expected Oliver to be out front waiting; he always was when she left him for any amount of time.

She checked her watch. It was late for him to still be napping, but early for eating. Rubbing the back of her neck, she headed for the back room. "Tante Marie? Sorry we're late."

From outside, Aimee heard the sound of Oliver's laughter. She smiled and turned to her father. "They're out back, Papa."

She pushed through the back door, stepped out onto the porch and stopped in shock. Oliver sat in his swing, the one that had been broken for weeks now, the one she had promised her son a dozen times that she would have fixed. It wasn't broken any more. And it wasn't Tante Marie standing behind Oliver, pushing him.

Aimee sucked in a sharp breath, fighting the instinct to race across the yard and yank Oliver off the swing—and away from Hunter. Instead, she stood and watched as Hunter swung Oliver higher than she had ever dared to. Oliver squealed with excitement; Hunter laughed in response. They looked good together. Happy. Like any other father and son enjoying each other's company on a pretty afternoon.

Only Oliver and Hunter weren't any other father and son. They never would be.

Oliver looked over his shoulder at Hunter, laughing, obviously begging him to push him harder, higher. Her heart turned over and she gripped the door frame for support. She couldn't have Oliver becoming attached to Hunter. Couldn't have him getting used to having Hunter around, depending on him. He would be hurt when Hunter left, or when Hunter wasn't there for him when he needed him most.

Just as Hunter had hurt her, just as he hadn't been there for her when she'd needed him most.

She wouldn't allow that to happen. She wouldn't allow Hunter the opportunity to hurt Oliver that way. Aimee caught her bottom lip between her teeth. But hadn't she already? She'd known how much Oliver loved swinging, how much he'd missed it. Why hadn't she followed through on her promise to have it fixed?

But maybe, Aimee acknowledged, if it hadn't been the swing that had brought them together, it would have been something else. For the first time since earlier that day, she thought of the scene she had witnessed between Oliver and Hunter that morning. Seeing them together like that, interacting on such a personal level, had caught her totally by surprise. She remembered thinking that there must be some mistake, that some sort of fluke had brought them together.

After all, Oliver and Hunter took care not to even look at each other.

She saw now it wasn't a one-time thing, wasn't a fluke.

What was she going to do?

Her father wheeled up behind her and for a moment, watched the father and son outside. Then he chuckled. "They look good together, *non?* They look happy."

Aimee glared at him, annoyed that he had mirrored her thoughts with words. "What you're seeing is an illusion. Hunter will never be a real father to Oliver, so stop hoping."

Roubin shook his head slowly. "No, *chère.* What I see is real. It is what you feel that is an illusion." Without waiting for a reply, he maneuvered himself around her and started down the ramp.

Aimee stared after him, tears stinging her eyes. Her feelings were real. Not imaginary. Not an illusion. She knew Hunter, understood him. It was her father, with his antiquated sense of family and duty, who was living in an imaginary world.

But if that were true, why did his words hurt so much?

Fighting the tears back, she marched after her father.

Oliver caught sight of them. "Pépère!" he cried. "Maman! Look, swing fixed!"

"I see that, baby," she said, forcing a smile. When she reached them, she stopped and looked furiously at Hunter. "You're pushing him too high," she said softly, carefully. "He's just a baby. He could be hurt."

"No, Maman!" Oliver pleaded, shaking his head. "Want to go higher!"

"I said no, Oliver. *I'm* the parent here. I know what's best for you."

"But, Maman—"

"Your mom's right, Tiger," Hunter interjected, slowing the swing, sending her a dark look as he did. "She's the boss and we follow orders. Right?"

Oliver stuck out his lower lip and sent her a sulky look. "Guess so."

Aimee's heart twisted. She and Oliver had always been a team. He was the light of her life, she of his. Nobody had ever come between them. Until this moment. Until Hunter.

Aimee placed her fists on her hips, shaking with anger and exhaustion. "Where's Tante Marie?"

"Cooking."

"Cooking?" Aimee echoed, surprised.

"Mmm. When it started to get late, she decided to get dinner going. She called cousin Alphonse and had him bring by some shrimp."

Cousin Alphonse? Aimee thought incredulously. Hunter said the name as if he were speaking of a member of his own family.

"She can't believe you haven't made me *étouffée* yet," he continued, grinning. "She clucked her tongue over that one."

Beside her, Roubin chuckled.

"Oh," Hunter added, giving Oliver a push, "a guy named Roberto called. He seemed pretty desperate to talk to you."

Aimee frowned, unsure which bothered her more— that Roberto wouldn't take no for an answer or that Hunter was acting like he'd moved in for good.

"Boyfriend?"

Aimee stiffened. "That's none of your business. You are a visitor here. Not one of the family. I didn't authorize you to watch my son or answer the phone or fix anything."

"Is something wrong, Aimee?" Hunter asked, his voice low, carefully controlled. "If there is, maybe you should just spit it out."

Aimee turned to her son, her nerves at the snapping point, a bubble of hysteria rising up in her. "Oliver, get down." When he defiantly shook his head, she sucked in a sharp breath, her control slipping one more notch. She knew she was acting irrationally, that her behavior was out of line, but she was too tired and too threatened to help herself. "Now!" she snapped.

Oliver's eyes filled and his lower lip began to quiver. Hunter stopped the swing, helped him off of it, then ruffled his hair. The familiarity of the gesture sent hysteria and insecurity charging through her. "Go get washed up for supper."

Oliver turned to Hunter as if for reassurance, and Hunter nodded. "Do what your mom says. We can swing more tomorrow."

"Come on, *petit-fils*. Pépère will give you a ride."

Aimee watched as Oliver gazed up at Hunter in adoration, and hysteria inched closer to the surface. How had everything changed so quickly? This morning Oliver wouldn't even look at Hunter, now he looked at him as if he were a god.

And what of Hunter? she thought, balling her hands into fists. Touching her son. Playing with him. Giving him direction as if he were Oliver's rightful parent.

Oliver climbed onto Roubin's lap, and they started for the house. Aimee saw that Marie had come out to see what the commotion was. Tears of frustration and embarrassment filled Aimee's eyes, and she swung back to Hunter. "Don't you ever presume to interfere with me and my son again. You have no right."

"Don't you think all this is a little uncalled-for? You're angry at me, don't drag Oliver into it. He wasn't doing anything but having fun."

"And what were you doing, Hunter? Having fun?"

He clenched his jaw. "What do *you* think, Aimee? Isn't that what this is really about?"

She flushed; she felt the color and cursed it. "He could have been hurt. You were acting irresponsibly, you—"

"He's not a baby, Aimee. He's a little boy. And maybe if you'd stop treating him as if he would break, he'd stop behaving as if he's afraid he will."

"What the hell is that supposed to mean?"

"Isn't that obvious, Aimee? You coddle him. You baby him. That's why he clings, why he's so shy. At the same age, Pete—"

Anger charged through her, and she took a step toward him. "Don't you compare Oliver to Pete. Not ever. They're different children. Besides, Oliver is doing great. If you'd ever really looked at him, you'd know that."

Tears sprang to her eyes, and feeling like an idiot she swung away from him. She fought for control, even as she felt it slipping.

Hunter moved up behind her and placed a hand on her shoulder. She knew he must feel her trembling. "You're exhausted," he murmured. "Go lay down."

"So you can win Oliver's love?" she snapped, swinging back around. "No way."

He drew his eyebrows together. "No. So you can rest." He lowered his voice and reached a hand out to her. "You look wiped out."

She slapped his hand away and had to fight to keep from slapping him again. "Thanks for the diagnosis, Doc. But I'm fine."

"I can see that," he said sarcastically, moving his gaze over her. "Paranoia becomes you."

He was right, damn him. She cocked her chin up. "Oliver is mine."

Hunter narrowed his eyes. "I told you, I have no ulterior motives."

"Then why are you here? Why were you . . . playing with him?"

"He wanted to swing. It was broken. I helped him out." Hunter expelled a frustrated, angry breath. "I have no intention of becoming Oliver's friend . . . or father."

Aimee brought a shaking hand to her head. She believed him; she believed he *thought* he meant what he said. But he hadn't watched the two of them together. He hadn't seen the way Oliver had looked at him, with adoration and a big case of hero worship. Nor had Hunter seen how relaxed and happy he had looked while pushing Oliver.

Aimee rubbed her temple. And he certainly hadn't been able to crawl inside her and feel how that terrified her. How guilty and inadequate it made her feel.

"Accept my offer," he coaxed. "And I'm gone."

She hesitated. All she had to do was say *yes*. And he would be gone. The threat of Oliver and Hunter becoming attached to each other would disappear. If he left, things could return to normal. *She* could return to normal.

But in the long run, wasn't the chance that Oliver would be hurt much greater?

She balled her hands into fists, fighting the tears that threatened. "I wish I could," she whispered, the sound choked with emotion and fatigue. "But I believe it's the wrong thing . . . to . . . do."

"Aimee—"

He reached out and touched her cheek. Tenderly but with infinite strength. She squeezed her eyes shut, fighting the urge to lean on him. The urge to rest her forehead against his chest and sob out her frustrations and fears, her exhaustion.

But if she did, he wouldn't be there for her.

"No, Hunter." She shook her head, her tears spilling over. "I . . ."

Unable to continue without totally embarrassing herself, she turned and ran for the house.

Light spilled out Hunter's open windows and into the darkness. Beckoning. Welcoming. Aimee hesitated just beyond the circle of light, a tray of food balanced in her hands. From inside, she heard strains of music, something moody and romantic, something that combined with the night sounds of the bayou to create a melancholy, heady sound.

Aimee cocked her head, listening, trying to make out the music's source. It came from neither the radio nor a tape; the sound reminded her of the jewelry box she'd had as a teenager. When she'd opened it, a tiny ballerina had pirouetted to a tune much like this one.

Aimee shook her head and stepped out of the darkness and into the light. She wasn't here to speculate on his choice of music or to wonder what he was doing, if he were thinking of her.

Or to wish for things that would never again be.

Aimee muttered an oath, annoyed with herself and the direction of her thoughts. She'd come to apologize for her earlier behavior and her wild accusations. And to bring him dinner. He hadn't shown up for the meal; she knew he'd stayed away to give her time to cool down.

She crossed quickly to his door and knocked. Get this over with, she told herself. Deliver the food and the apology, then leave. No fuss, no muss. No embarrassing scenes or almost embraces.

Hunter opened the door and Aimee's resolve of a moment before evaporated like a breath of cool air in July. Hunter stood before her, his gloriously male body unclothed save for a pair of running shorts.

Her pulse scrambled, and even as Aimee told herself to keep her eyes on his face, she lowered them. She hadn't forgotten how beautiful he was, nor had time embellished her memories of him. He was subtly muscled and strong; he had the body of a man who had been active all his life. His skin was tan and firm and would be warm against her hands, becoming hot when sexually aroused. His broad shoulders and chest tapered down to narrow hips and a flat, hard stomach. A dusting of golden hair covered his chest, forming a vee that disappeared beneath the waistband of his low-slung shorts.

Aimee followed the line of the vee with her eyes, stopping when she realized just what she was looking at. She jerked her gaze up to his, her cheeks hot with color.

Although he said nothing, a smile tugged at his mouth. He knew exactly what she was thinking, what she was feeling. The heat in her cheeks became fire. She cursed both the color and her response to him.

She took a deep breath. "May I come in?"

For a split second she sensed hesitation in him, then he swung the door wider. "Sure."

Aimee moved past him and into his room. She'd seen this room hundreds of times before, but tonight it looked different to her. It *felt* different. As if his presence had changed it, charged the atmosphere with his own personal energy.

That energy crackled along her nerve endings, heightening each of her senses. She could smell the subtle male scent of him, that of his spicy soap in the bathroom, the yeasty scent of beer. She could feel the warmth of his body and the gentle breeze kicked up by the fan above, could hear her own thundering heart, his even breathing.

Dear Lord, she was losing it. She told herself the room was no different than it had been last week, that she was still exhausted, that she was coming down with something.

She didn't believe her own reassurances. Everything was changed. She was changed.

Aimee turned her gaze to him. She tried to smile and failed miserably. "I brought you ... dinner," she said. "Marie's *étouffée* is the best in the parish—it would be a shame to miss it. Besides, I don't think she'd ever forgive me if you did."

A ghost of a smile touched his mouth and he took the tray. "She takes good cooking seriously."

"It wasn't just that." Aimee met his eyes, then looked uncomfortably away. "She thinks you're the best thing since cayenne pepper. She spent the entire meal talking about your visit."

"Sorry I missed that," he said solemnly. "Obviously, she doesn't know me the way you do." Turning, Hunter placed the tray on the bed, then faced her once more. "You didn't have to do this, Aimee."

"Yes ... I did." She slipped her hands into the front pockets of her shorts. "But your missed dinner isn't the only reason I'm here. I wanted to ... apologize for earlier. I was out of line."

"Forget it."

"I can't. I need to ... get this off my chest." She cleared her throat. "You were right, I was exhausted. Today was a nightmare and when I came home and found you and Oliver having such a ... good time together, my imagination took wing and I just lost it. I'm sorry."

Hunter reached out and touched her cheek, just once and lightly, then dropped his hand. "You're human."

The urge to cry hit her so hard it took away her breath. For the second time in a matter of hours she wanted to lean in to him, wanted him to hold her and stroke her; she wanted him to absorb her tears and give her his strength.

Instead, she folded her arms across her chest and held tightly to her control. "And I wanted to thank you for fixing Oliver's swing. I kept promising him and putting it off. I feel bad about that."

"You can't do everything."

"No? Sometimes it seems like there's no one el..." Her voice cracked and she choked the words back, forcing a weak smile. "Never mind. I guess I'll be going so you can eat before it gets cold."

"Don't go," Hunter said, catching her arm. She stopped and met his eyes. "I want to show you something."

He released her arm and crossed the room to retrieve the music box. As he picked it up, he glanced back at her. Standing in the soft light of his lamp, she looked younger than she was and heartbreakingly lonely. How had he ever let her go?

Hunter shook his head at the thought. It had been for the best. It still was. Most times, the reasoning of the mind hadn't a thing to do with the gut. And even less control over it.

Hunter carried the box to her and held it out. She looked at it, then up at him, surprised. "It's beautiful."

Hunter gazed at her, taking in the features that were unconventionally beautiful—the almost exotically almond-shaped eyes, the nose that turned up on the end, the too-full mouth that had fascinated him endlessly.

The beauty of the music box, of its belle inside, couldn't hold a candle to Aimee's. "Yes," he murmured. "Beautiful."

Her cheeks grew pink. "It doesn't look like something... you would own."

"I know." He smiled, still amazed by his own behavior. "That's exactly what I was thinking as I shelled out an exorbitant amount of money for it."

Aimee reached out and touched the glass lightly. "Just before I knocked, I heard music. This was it?"

"Yes." He wound the key and the melody surrounded them.

Aimee was quiet for a moment. "Why are you showing me this?"

He didn't know, that was the damnable part. Just as he hadn't been certain why he'd bought it in the first place. It had just felt like the right thing to do. He wasn't accustomed to acting on impulse or feelings. He found the fact that he had unnerving.

"Because," he answered finally, "it's one of the things that brought me here."

She drew her eyebrows together. "Then I suppose I should despise it."

"But you can't."

"It's too beautiful." She took the box from his hands and crossed to the light to look at it more closely.

Hunter followed, stopping directly behind her. If she leaned back just a fraction, she would rest against his naked chest. Even though she held herself ramrod straight, he could imagine the weight of her against him, imagine the feel of her fragrant hair against his fingers.

He reached around her to touch the box. As he did, his arm brushed against her cheek. "I felt compelled to buy it," he murmured. "Just as I felt compelled to come here to see you."

She looked over her shoulder at him, searching his gaze with her own, her eyes full of questions. She left them unasked and turned back to the music box.

"Look," he said, touching the dome's glass. "Night jasmine. In the belle's hands. The shopkeeper pointed it out. I remembered you telling me about it."

"Yes," she whispered, looking back at him once more. "I remember, too. It's potent tonight."

"Yes."

Their gazes met and held. The room grew suddenly too warm, too still. The smell of the jasmine surrounded them, almost overpowering in its sweetness. Her lips trembled and she lowered her eyes to his mouth. Hunter leaned toward her.

Aimee took a step back. "I have to go." She set the music box on the bed and started for the door.

He caught her hand. "Stay."

She shook her head. "I can't. I—"

"Please." He laced their fingers. "I've always hated eating alone. Yet I almost always do."

He had her with that. He saw the empathy, the understanding soften her eyes. Still, she hesitated a moment more. "Oliver—"

"Is no doubt asleep. And Roubin is the last person you want to be with right now."

"Unfair," she whispered. "You know me too well."

Hunter smiled. "Yeah, but you have the same advantage."

She smiled then, a gentle curving of her lips that he felt like a punch to his gut. Hunter retrieved the tray and carried it out to the porch. They sat side-by-side on the steps. The air was warm, heavy with both moisture and the scent of the jasmine. In the distance they heard the hoot of an owl, the cry of an egret; closer to them, the song of the crickets and the sound of their own breathing.

Hunter uncovered his food, he smelled the sting of the spice a moment before he tasted it. "This is delicious."

"It's probably cold."

"It doesn't matter. It's still wonderful."

"I'll tell Tante Marie you said so." Aimee drew her knees to her chest and stared out at the darkness. Minutes passed with neither of them speaking.

Hunter thought of all the times they had sat together like this, quietly but with a sort of unspoken communication. Tonight, the atmosphere between them was one of awkward truce and uncomfortable awareness. He cursed the loss even as he accepted blame for it.

"Tell me about today, Aimee," he murmured, needing to break the silence. "What happened?"

She tipped her face to his, then looked away again, gazing across the yard to her home. "Papa's not making the kind of progress he should be, and the therapist thought that if he watched us work together he could help us correct any problems we were having."

A touch of bitterness colored her tone. "Of course, all we're having are problems."

She sighed and rested her chin on her drawn-up knees. "The therapist supervised while I worked with him. It was awful. Papa fought me, fought the physical therapist when he tried to intervene. He refused to cooperate on any level."

Hunter set his plate aside and covered one of her hands with his own. He hated to see her despair. Her bitterness. They were so foreign to the woman he had known before. It saddened him to see her so unhappy.

"Every time I touched him," she continued, "he complained. Or criticized. I couldn't do anything right." She breathed in, the sound shaky and aching. "It hurt. It was humiliating to be treated that way in front of a stranger. I felt like a fool. Like an incompetent, uncaring daughter."

Hunter moved his thumb gently across her knuckles. He should ask her why she allowed her father to treat her that way. He should give her the advice he knew she needed, should tell her that was exactly how her father wanted her to feel, at least on a subconscious level.

But he didn't want a confrontation, not tonight. He wanted to comfort her. He wanted to be there for her. "I'm sorry."

She lifted her lips in a small smile, then tilted her face up to the star-strewn sky. "You should have seen Papa before his illness. Big and strapping. Confident. Full of life and strength." She laughed, the sound full of love. "When I was a little girl, he was my hero. Maybe all little girls say that of their fathers, but Papa, with his booming voice and deep, rich laugh, was so much larger than life to me. In my eyes he could do nothing wrong. I remember just looking up at him and being filled with . . . awe."

"And he doted on you."

"Yes. I was his little girl, his only child. He thought I was perfect." She frowned then, and slipped her hand from his. She dropped her right hand to the old wooden step and ran her finger back and forth across its surface, grooved and scarred with age. "I'm not certain when it began to go wrong. Maybe when Maman died. Maybe when I began to see that he was a man, not a hero."

Hunter caught her hand again, this time lacing their fingers. "Maybe it didn't go wrong," he murmured. "Maybe it just changed. Relationships do."

"Maybe." She gazed down at their joined hands, then looked back up at him. "He's never forgiven me for leaving. Nothing I can do now seems to be able to make up for that betrayal. But I only knew I had to go. That this life—his life—wasn't the one I wanted."

"Yet, here you are."

His comment hurt her; he could see it in her eyes. He hadn't meant to, but as he'd murmured the words he'd known that they would. After all, how could they not? She was the same woman who had left home all those years ago, she had the same dreams, although he knew she would deny it.

He brought their joined hands to his mouth and pressed his lips to hers. "You didn't betray him, Aimee. You did what you had to. You followed your dream."

She pulled her hand away. "I was young. So naive and starry-eyed."

He cupped her face. "You were brash and self-confident. You had everything going for you."

"Not enough, apparently. Illusions. Dreams of grandeur."

"No, Aimee. You're wrong."

She placed her hands on his bare chest, suddenly angry. Beneath her palms, his heart thundered. "Not enough going for me to keep the critics from ripping me to shreds. Not enough to keep you."

"I didn't leave."

She laughed, the sound brittle to her own ears. "But you were never really there, Hunter. *I* was our relationship. The only thing that kept us together as long as we were was my naive belief that I could shape the world and everyone in it. Including you."

He moved one of his hands to the back of her neck, circling it with his fingers. A wild, irrational anger flared inside him. "I was there. More than you know."

"How?" she demanded, curling her hands into fists on his chest. "In bed? And if so, how do I know if it was even me you were with?"

He swore. "How could you even doubt it?"

"How could I not?"

He swore again and dragged her against his chest. "Because I never felt with anyone the way I did with you. Even Ginny. I died a hundred agonizing, guilty deaths because of that, but I couldn't change it."

"Well, that makes me feel just great," she said, the words tight with fury. "Even when we made love, she was on your mind. You felt like you were cheating on her."

She started to stand; he pulled her back down to him. He cupped the back of her head. "Damn you, Aimee, that's not what I meant."

"No? I can't see it any other way. You felt guilty, like you were cheating on your wi—"

Hunter silenced her with his mouth. His kiss dominated, it bruised. She didn't resist; instead she met his force, matched his fury. She parted her lips—his tongue found hers, mating with it. He caught both her hands in one of his and tumbled her back against the porch floor.

Hunter lifted his head and gazed down at her. Her eyes were smoky with arousal, her cheeks wild with color. He lowered his eyes to her mouth, soft with passion, parted in invitation. He moved his gaze lower still, his arousal painful. Her full breasts pressed against the light cotton of her blouse, her nipples stood out, erect and—he knew—aching for his hands, his mouth.

He'd seen her this way dozens of times before; it felt like the first. As if a dying man, Hunter greedily took her mouth once more, cupping her breasts with hands greedier still, molding, caressing.

Aimee arched into his hands, wanting more, needing everything. It had been so long. So very long. She bit back a moan as he moved a hand lower, over her rib cage, her abdomen, to the apex of her thighs. He curved his fingers around her. She arched up, crying out with pleasure and shock.

Hunter caught her cry with his mouth. "Remember, Aimee?" he rasped. "Remember how it was between us?"

She did. So well it was like yesterday. Yet at the same time, she had forgotten what it was to be alive, to be a whole woman. Sexual. Sensual. Complete.

Aimee reveled in the sensation, in the excitement roaring through her, fighting off the other memories. Memories of pain. Memories of the devastation she had felt at the end, when she had finally realized he would never love her.

With a sound of pain, Aimee flattened her hands against his chest and pushed. "No, Hunter."

He lifted his head, his hands from her body. He gazed down at her, out of breath, his eyes dark with desire. For one moment, she felt herself weakening, her muscles liquefying once more with arousal, then she firmed her resolve. "Let me up."

He rolled off her and she jumped to her feet. "I've got to go."

He followed her to her feet; he caught her hand, lacing their fingers. "Don't go. Stay with me." He lowered his voice to a caress. "You want to."

She did, she wanted to so badly she ached. But if she stayed she would regret it forever. "I can't." She shook her head for emphasis. "I can't."

"Then why did you come to me tonight?"

Her cheeks heated with anger, and she narrowed her eyes. "Cheap shot, Hunter. You know I didn't come here for that." She tugged against his grasp. "It's over between us."

"No." He dragged her against his chest. "It's not over. You can feel it between us, Aimee. It's still there."

"What you feel between us," she said, struggling for control, "could be taken care of by any woman."

"You'd like to believe that, wouldn't you? Just as you'd like to believe that any man has the ability to make you feel the way I do." He slid his hands to her bottom, cupping her, drawing her against his arousal. "I haven't been with anyone else, Aimee. Not since you left."

His words, their meaning, rocketed through her. He hadn't made love with another woman. She must have meant something to him. She must have been important. Special.

But not important enough. Not special enough to love.

She balled her hands into fists against his chest. "Why are you doing this? Do you believe you have something to give me this time? Something more than sex and a place to live and make my photographs? And what of Oliver? Where does he fit in the scenario? Do you have anything to give him?"

Hunter swore and swung away from her. For long moments he stared out at the darkness. Then he turned back to her. "Doesn't what I said mean anything to you? Doesn't the fact that I haven't been able to forget you, that I haven't desired another woman since you, mean anything?"

She drew in a shuddering breath. "It means you're a faithful man, Hunter Powell. But I already knew that. After all, you haven't loved anyone since Ginny and Pete." She met his gaze, hope trembling inside her. "Have you?"

Hunter took a step away from her. It hurt to hear her say Ginny's and Pete's names. It hurt to know she was right. He wanted Aimee to give him everything. He wanted to knock down her walls, wanted to peel away all her protective layers, force her to face... What? Her need for him? Her own fears and pain?

Yet, what was he willing to give in return? What did he have to give her?

"Don't worry, darling, everything will be fine. Just hurry home...."

"I love you, Daddy...."

"Is this your son, Mr. Powell? And this, is this your wife?"

Ginny... Pete... Dear God, no...

Hunter squeezed his eyes shut against the memories, the images that tumbled after them. "You're right," he said, his voice choked with pain. He turned away from her, struggling to submerge the memories, not wanting her to see the extent of his anguish. "I don't have anything to give you."

Aimee took a step toward him, her hand outstretched. "Hunter, I want to understand. I—"

"Just go," he said, not turning. "I'm a dead man. Save yourself."

With a muffled sound of pain, she did.

Chapter Six

The next morning, Aimee and Oliver were gone. Aimee had left a basket of breakfast pastries, some homemade preserves and a note. Hunter picked it up and scanned its contents. She'd taken Oliver to mass, then to a cousin's to play for the day. She would try to be home by suppertime, but if not, there were leftovers in the refrigerator.

Hunter frowned at the generic message. It was addressed to neither him nor Roubin, although he couldn't imagine that Aimee hadn't talked to her father before she left. So, she'd meant it for him.

He reread the message, his frown deepening. The impersonality of the note shouldn't bother him. He told himself it didn't.

But that was a lie. It bothered the hell out of him.

Hunter curled his fingers around the paper, crushing it. After what had occurred between them the night before, he wanted, expected, something personal. Something emotional—even if only anger.

Dammit, he hadn't been able to sleep for thinking of her, for brooding over what had happened between them, brooding over how it had made him feel.

He wasn't supposed to be feeling anything.

Hunter pocketed the wadded paper, then helped himself to a couple biscuits and a mug of coffee. Thankfully, Roubin was nowhere to be seen. He had no desire to make small talk with the other man this morning.

Hunter took his breakfast and crossed the yard to his own small porch. He made himself comfortable on the steps, his mind flooding with the image of Aimee as she'd been the night before: her eyes dark with arousal, her mouth soft and bruised from his own.

Only a matter of hours ago, he thought. She'd been here with him. In his arms. Only a matter of hours ago, he'd felt alive. And for one brief moment, ridiculously hopeful.

Hunter swore and set aside his biscuits, his appetite gone. What was wrong with him? What kind of man was he, to want Aimee to admit her feelings for him when he had nothing to give her in return? What kind of person was he, to want her so badly when he knew another affair between them would only end in a dead-end for her?

He had nothing to offer her. Nothing to offer Oliver.

Across the way, he saw Roubin wheel out of his house. The older man didn't see Hunter, and Hunter watched as Roubin progressed slowly across the yard on the paved path that had been put in specifically for that purpose.

He handled the chair clumsily, as if he hadn't gotten used to it yet. Hunter drew his eyebrows together. Roubin had suffered his aneurysm before Aimee returned from California, and she'd returned nearly four years ago. Roubin should be a whiz in the chair by now.

Unless he'd refused to grow accustomed to it.

Hunter's mouth lifted. Maybe he did have something to give Aimee and Oliver. Not the emotional commitment they deserved, but he was a doctor, after all. A healer. His clinic specialized in rehabilitation from the aftereffects of catastrophic illness.

But before he could do anything, he would have to speak with Roubin's physician. What was the man's name? Aimee had mentioned it the morning she'd cut her hand. *Landrieu...Landers...* Hunter searched his memory for the name. *Landry.* That was it. *Dr. Landry.*

Hunter stood, excited at the prospect of helping Aimee and Roubin. Too excited to wait until Monday to act on his decision. Even though it was Sunday, he felt certain Landry would take the time to speak with him. As a professional courtesy. And because, if the physician was worth his salt, he was probably as frustrated with Roubin as Aimee was.

After calling out a greeting to Roubin, Hunter went in search of a phone book.

In the gathering twilight, Roubin sat alone. Hunter stood at the end of the wheelchair path, studying the older man. Motionless, his hands folded in his lap, Roubin stared off into the distance. Around him, the bayou prepared for night. Roubin seemed not to notice, seemed disconnected from all but his own isolation.

How long had he been sitting there? Hunter wondered, starting down the path. An hour? Two? All day? Compassion tugged at him. He supposed it shouldn't. Because of his profession, because he knew that Roubin had the ability to create or end his own alienation.

But how could he not feel for him? In many ways he and Roubin were alike—they were both lost men.

A chameleon scurried across the path in front of him, diving into the foliage on the other side. Hunter increased his pace, wanting the opportunity to speak with Roubin before Oliver and Aimee returned home.

"Good evening," Hunter said, as he reached the house. He stopped at the bottom of the stairs and smiled up at the older man. "How about some company?"

Roubin nodded and motioned for Hunter to come and sit beside him. Hunter did, and for several moments they sat in silence. Roubin broke it first. "Aimee and Oliver, they are not home yet." He shook his head and lifted his face to the breeze, frowning. "And a storm, she comes."

Hunter looked up at the cloudless evening sky. "I didn't hear anything about bad weather on the radio."

Roubin made a sound of disdain. "Those Yankees, they go to school to learn about the weather. What can they know by looking at charts and numbers? *Non.*

Feel the air." The old man lifted a hand to the breeze. "She is alive. And listen. It is too quiet. The birds and the crickets, where have they gone? I do not hear them. The bayou, too, is quiet. She seems to be waiting."

Hunter sat still, trying to tune in to what Roubin referred. Finally, he shook his head. "Sorry."

Roubin laughed. "Do not worry, you are new to this place. Me, all my life, I have to rely on my senses. To make my living, to protect my family. Just once you forget, and maybe you don't come home that night.

"I know men like this," he continued. "Men who watch the television to know what the Mother Nature, she is planning. Their wives become widows." He shook his head. "It is very sad."

Roubin narrowed his eyes, gazing toward the road. "I was the best on the bayou. Mother Nature, I outwit her every time." His mouth thinned suddenly, bitterly. "But my own body, like the *gros farceur,* it tricks me."

"But you're alive," Hunter murmured. "You're lucky."

Roubin scowled. "Luck, eh? That is what you call this? Chained to this chair, unable to be a man?"

"Some of those chains are of your own making." Hunter met the other man's gaze. "I talked to Dr. Landry today."

Roubin's dark eyes blackened with temper. "That *imposteur?* What does he know?"

"Quite a lot," Hunter said easily. "Judging by our conversation."

"Bon Dieu!" Roubin slapped his palm down on the chair's arm. "This was not your right to do."

"Maybe not." Hunter glanced at the darkening sky, feeling for the first time the change in the air. A storm was indeed coming. He looked back at the other man. "You know I'm a doctor?"

"*Oui.*"

Roubin's expression communicated to Hunter just what he thought of that bit of information. Undaunted, Hunter continued. "I run a clinic that specializes in physical rehabilitation. Many of our patients are victims of strokes and aneurysms, most have problems like yours."

Roubin grunted. "And what do you think this means to me?"

"Dr. Landry believes there's a good chance you could walk again. After speaking with him, I agree with his prognosis."

"Walk with a cane," Roubin murmured bitterly. "Or a walker. What good would I be to Aimee? To my *petit-fils?*"

"What good are you to them now?" Hunter said baldly. "Bound to that chair by your own bitterness and self-pity. Why, Roubin? What exactly are you afraid of?"

The older man's face reddened with fury. "What do you know about my life? About what I feel in my heart?" Roubin balled his hands into fists. "You are a stranger to me. To my family. Go home. You do not belong here."

"No, I don't belong here. And I don't know you. But I know Aimee. I know she wishes, in her heart, to be somewhere else, but stays out of guilt. I know she needs some help around here. You know these things, too."

Swearing in French, Roubin began to turn his chair toward the door. "What if Dr. Landry's wrong?" Hunter asked. "What if you can do better than a cane or walker?"

Roubin stopped and turned to meet Hunter's eyes.

"Doctors don't know everything," Hunter continued. "I could be kicked out of the profession for saying so, but I'm saying it anyway. When it comes to the human spirit, the will to live or succeed, there's a hell of a lot doctors don't know."

Roubin didn't reply, but he didn't move either.

"I learned early," Hunter went on. "I was a first-year resident. There was a patient, a woman, who had suffered a basal brain aneurysm. Similar to yours. She'd been in a deep coma several months. One day, while on rounds with the lead doctor, we ran into the patient's daughter. The doctor berated the woman for not having signed a 'no emergency measures' form, for holding on to delusions he said helped no one. He announced to us, in front of the family member and the patient, that the patient was severely brain damaged and even should she come out of the coma, she would be a vegetable. His words.

"The next day, that patient did come out of her coma. She opened her eyes and asked for mashed potatoes and gravy."

"Non." Roubin laughed and shook his head. "This is true?"

"Absolutely. The experience changed me forever." Hunter smiled, remembering the look on the lead doctor's face when he'd heard the news. "The medical journals, the newspapers and magazines are filled with stories of people who are told they will never walk again, never run again, never live normally again, yet for some inexplicable reason they're able to do just that.

"Doctors like to discount these stories. Not because we want to be gods, but because, like God, so often we hold life and death in our hands. That's a damn frightening proposition, even without the element of the unexplainable. Science and our unshakable belief in the laws of science is our security blanket."

"And you?"

Hunter lifted his shoulders. "I don't know." He smiled. "Colleagues have been known to call me odd."

Thunder rumbled in the distance. Roubin looked uneasily up at the darkening sky, then back at Hunter. "What you are telling me, what does it mean?"

"That what happens to you is *up* to you, Roubin. Only you can determine how far you can go in your rehabilitation."

For long moments Roubin gazed silently down at his hands. Then he looked back up at Hunter. "But I could try my best and never walk again. Dr. Landry, he could be right."

"True. But you would have lost nothing." Hunter crossed to the older man, stopping in front of him. Hunter thought of Ginny, of Pete, of the senselessness of their deaths. "You lived, Roubin. You're alive. Life means something. It's worth something."

Roubin nodded solemnly. "*Le bon Dieu,* he has a plan."

Hunter motioned to Roubin's chair. "Is this it? Is this his plan for you? To sit and wish for a different life, to spend your days cursing fate? You're alive, but you have no life."

Roubin stared at him. "You are a religious man?"

Hunter paused, then shook his head. "I used to be."

Roubin seemed to consider that for a moment. "You speak plainly."

Hunter smiled. "I've been accused of that before."

"Bon." Roubin drew his heavy eyebrows together. "I will think about what you have said to me."

"Do that." Hunter took a step back. "And while you are, think about this as well—I'd like to take a look at your legs myself. I'd like to take you through a round of your PT exercises, to evaluate myself. Let me know if you'd be willing to—"

"Oui."

Hunter stopped, surprised. He hadn't expected Roubin to agree so quickly. In truth, he hadn't expected him to agree at all. Excitement pumped through him. Until that moment, he hadn't realized just how much he wanted to help the other man.

"Now?" he asked.

Roubin nodded. "You have the time?"

"You bet." Hunter smiled and motioned toward the door. "After you."

Aimee and Oliver arrived home as the first drops of rain splashed against the windshield. All the way from Thibodaux it had been on her heels and Aimee had pushed the speed limit, hoping they could beat it. This one looked as if it were going to be a doozy.

"Come on, baby, we're going to have to hurry," she said, helping Oliver from the car and glancing uneasily up at the dark, rumbling sky. "Hold on."

Oliver obediently wrapped his arms and legs around Aimee and she started for the chair path, moving as quickly as she could with his added weight.

Her father had left all the lights on and the house glowed with warm, welcoming light. He would be worried; she should have called. Aimee frowned, acknowledging her ridiculous attempt at rebellion. She'd deliberately stayed late. She hadn't returned home in time for dinner because she'd wanted to avoid seeing Hunter. She hadn't called because she hadn't wanted Hunter to know her agenda.

And because she . . . just hadn't wanted to call.

Her father had known where she was; if he'd been really worried he could have called. He hadn't.

A fat drop of rain hit her cheek. With Oliver in her arms, she couldn't reach up to wipe it and it rolled down her face like a tear. In the light of her behavior of the night before, it had been difficult to face the dawn. Her head had been full of the way she'd reacted to Hunter's kiss and touch. Like a woman starved for sex. Like a wanton.

How could she have behaved so?

Even now, her cheeks heated. Aimee shook her head, fighting back the wave of embarrassment and self-recriminations. She could do nothing about the past, so she wouldn't dwell on it.

But she could control the future.

She'd realized that sometime during the day. At the same moment she'd remembered that Hunter was a transient in all their lives. That before long he would be gone and life would resume its normal pace.

The thought brought an ache, and she scolded herself for it. She wanted her life back. She did. A day without Hunter had cleared her head. When she was with him she couldn't think clearly, couldn't separate real feelings from leftovers from the past.

A crash of thunder shook the night, a brilliant flash of light on its heels. Aimee reached the house just as the sky opened up. She climbed the steps to the gallery, then set Oliver down. She motioned to the end of the gallery and his new tricycle. "Quick, baby, get your bike before it gets wet."

He scurried down the gallery, and Aimee opened the front door, ready to call out. The greeting died on her tongue. She hadn't avoided Hunter. He was here, squatted beside the wheelchair holding one of her father's legs, gently bending and straightening it. Beside the chair she saw her father's exercise platform set up.

Aimee frowned, confused. What was he . . .

She caught her breath as she realized Hunter was taking her father through one of his PT exercises; it looked as if they had done an entire round. And her father was cooperating. She drew her eyebrows together. In fact, he wasn't just allowing Hunter to work with him, he was helping Hunter. Working with him. He had a look of concentration, of effort, on his face.

Several emotions collided inside her. Disbelief. Surprise and hurt. An overwhelming sense of betrayal.

Aimee shook her head, tears stinging her eyes. Her father had never gone along with her, not the way he was with Hunter. He'd fought her every time. He'd made it difficult and uncomfortable for them both. Grueling, even.

Yet here he was now, letting a stranger work his legs without a murmur of protest.

As if sensing her presence, Hunter looked up. Their eyes met and the tears in hers brimmed. Damn him, she thought. He knew exactly what she was thinking and feeling, she could see it in his eyes.

At that moment, Oliver barreled past her and through the door. *"Pépère!"*

Roubin looked up, his eyes bright and for the first time in what seemed like forever, full of life and hope. Aimee stared at him in stunned surprise, the feeling of betrayal deepening.

Laughter tumbled from her father, rich and deep, and he clapped his hands and held out his arms. Oliver ran to him and launched himself onto his lap.

Aimee drew in a quick, shocked breath. She gripped the door frame, the thunder booming outside no match for the thunder of her heart. In that moment her father looked as he had before his illness, before the two of them had begun to argue. Before she had left La Fin.

Hunter had made him look like that. For three and a half years she had tried and failed. The failure curled through her, tightening in her chest, squeezing her heart.

"Guess what, Pépère?" Oliver said, twisting in his grandfather's lap. "I rode pony t'day. She try to make me fall off, but I didn't!"

Oliver turned his excited gaze to Hunter. "Should have seen! Maman was scared, but not Oliver! You come next time? Be real fun."

Even her son was turning to Hunter, Aimee thought, making a sound of pain. Coming out of himself in a way he never had before—in a way she'd never been able to make him feel secure enough to do.

Unable to face her failure any longer, she turned and strode out onto the gallery. She snapped the door shut behind her, not caring what her father or anyone else thought of her behavior.

She moved to the darkest part of the gallery. The rain had eased momentarily but the wind had picked up, and she turned, facing into it, finding comfort in its angry strength. It pulled at her hair and clothes, the drops of rain stinging her cheeks. But still she faced it, staring at the strobe-lit sky, wishing for something as brilliant and intangible as the flashes of lightning, something just as far from her reach.

"Aimee."

At the sound of Hunter's voice, she squeezed her eyes shut. Why had he followed her tonight when so many other times he hadn't? Why tonight, when she would prefer to be alone?

He called her name again.

Turning slowly, she met his eyes. For long moments, she just gazed at him. The lightning illuminated his face crazily; at one moment his expression was drenched in darkness, the next bathed in light. The lighting made him at one moment tangible, approachable, the next an enigma, mysterious and out of reach.

She turned away from him, choosing instead to face the wind. "You can't imagine," she said finally, softly, "how I felt when I opened the door and saw you and Papa working together. When I saw that you had been able to accomplish immediately and seemingly without effort what I had been unable to in years. You can't imagine how much that hurt."

She glanced over her shoulder at him. He stood immobile, as if planted to the gallery, legs slightly spread, arms at his side. In that moment, ridiculously, he reminded her of the old oak tree in the yard. Strong and rooted, a shelter in a storm. She reminded herself that Hunter was neither of those things and called herself a fool.

"I feel so betrayed." She sucked in a deep breath. "For nearly four years I've tried to work with him. He hasn't let me. He hasn't cooperated. Yet you come here, a stranger, nobody to him, and he works with you." Her voice broke. "He smiles like I haven't seen him smile in forever. He laughs."

"And that's bad?" Hunter closed the distance between them. "I thought you'd be happy to see your father progress."

She swore, guilt curling through her. "I am happy. I do want him to progress."

"But only if you're the one doing the helping. Is that it?"

"Bastard."

She pushed by him; he caught her elbow, stopping her, forcing her to meet his eyes. "Snap out of it, Aimee. Self-pity doesn't become you. And it certainly isn't helping your father."

The adrenaline of fury began to pump through her. "What do you know abou—"

"I talked to Dr. Landry today."

Aimee stared at him for a moment, surprised silent. "You did what?"

"You heard me." A ghost of a smile touched his mouth. "Nice man. Seems to be a good doctor."

"I can't believe you had the audacity—"

"Believe it."

The urge to hit him was so strong it took her breath away. She fought it off even as she inched her chin up, ready to do verbal battle. "And what did *my* father's doctor tell you?"

"That you coddle Roubin. That he could walk again if he was willing to work for it. If he had a reason to work for it."

Aimee clenched her hands into fists. "I know that. My father knows that. But he refuses to do what he has to."

"Why should he? You do everything for him."

She drew in a deep breath, using the moment to try to garner a shred of control. "I don't have to listen to this. And I won't. This conversation is over, Hunter."

Again she began to move past him, and again he stopped her. "I'm not trying to hurt you, Aimee. Quite to the contrary, I'm trying to help. These are things you need to hear."

"Things you, in your infinite wisdom, have deemed it necessary I hear. You are arrogant beyond belief." She jerked against his grasp. "Now, let me go."

Hunter tightened his grip instead, narrowing his eyes in determination. "Stop coddling your father, Aimee.

Stop acting out of some sort of misplaced guilt. You're going to have to get tough. You're going to have to force him to be self-reliant. He's using you, manipulating you with your own guilt. You're letting him because you're afraid. Of what I'm not quite sure. But I am sure that neither of you is doing the other a damn bit of good."

"How dare you! How—"

"And what about Oliver?" Hunter demanded, drawing her closer to him, so close she had to tip her head back to meet his eyes. "What about how this situation is affecting him?"

"Leave my son out of this." She flattened her hands on Hunter's chest, denying that his words touched any chord of truth, or concern, inside her. "Oliver's fine."

"Right." Hunter laughed, the harsh sound mocking her. "Fine. He's got a mother with a martyr complex and a grandfather who's given up the world of the living."

"What do you know about us?" she cried. "About the way I feel about my father? About what my son needs?"

"Plenty." Hunter lowered his voice. "I've seen this type of family scenario played out a hundred times before. I deal with patients like Roubin and daughters like you every day. The scripts vary, but the premise is always the same."

Fury flashed through her, as hot and white as the lightning above. "You self-important bastard! You accuse me of acting out of guilt! What about you? Isn't guilt the whole reason you're here?"

Hunter flinched but when he continued, his tone was as even and hard as tempered steel. "Your father feels sorry for himself. You feel sorry for him, too. But maybe even sorrier for yourself. You feel responsible. And guilty. As if somehow you could have prevented this from happening. As if somehow, if you'd been a better daughter—"

"Stop it!" She balled her hands into fists against his chest. "How can you be so cold? How could I ever have felt anything for you?"

"It hurts you to see him incapacitated and unhappy. So you let him manipulate you. You do things for him that he's capable of doing for himself, that he *should* be doing for himself, all in the name of being there for him. You're making it easy for him. And hard. Take it from a professional and an impartial observer—lose the guilt, Slick."

Impartial observer. Those words hurt more than any others he'd said tonight. Because they were true. Even when they'd been lovers he'd been an observer instead of a participant in their relationship.

"What do you know about being there for someone?" she asked, her voice choked with a combination of tears and fury. "About really caring what happens to them? When was the last time you did either? When you kissed your wife goodbye that final time?"

Swearing, Hunter swung away from her. He crossed to the edge of the gallery and stared out at the darkness. When he spoke, his tone was low and almost devoid of emotion. "We're not talking about me, Aimee."

She crossed to him. Gripping his arm, she forced him to look at her. "We never do, do we? You never let anyone in or close. You wouldn't want to be touched, right? You wouldn't want to actually *feel* something?"

A muscle jumped in his jaw, and he narrowed his eyes. Aimee saw that he was angry and that he struggled to control the emotion.

"At least I'm not hiding," he said softly, viciously. "You're unhappy here, yet you stay. What are you hiding from, Aimee? Rejection? Fear of success?"

"Hiding? Me?" She tipped her head back and laughed, the hard sound ripped away from her by the wind. "You've been hiding since Ginny and Pete's death. Even though we were lovers, you never talked to me about the fire or how you felt. So often I would see your pain, yet you were never willing to share it with me. Just as you never shared any other part of yourself."

Tears welled in her eyes once again, for his pain, for her own. "Everything I learned about Ginny and Pete, I learned from other people. But even so, I knew you well enough to know you wished you'd died with them. That in a way you had. Isn't that so, Hunter?"

She saw the pain in his eyes, the regrets, the bitter longings. She wished she saw denial of her words instead. She wished he could look at her and pronounce himself alive and free. A cry of despair rose to her lips; it came out as a whimper. When was she going to stop wishing for the impossible and get on with the possible?

With a deafening crack of thunder, the sky unleashed a flood. The wind blew the rain onto the gallery, soaking their clothes, their hair and skin.

Still they stood, so close their bodies brushed as they worked to keep their balance against the wind. From inside, Aimee heard Oliver's shriek of amusement, her father's deep laughter. Around her, the storm howled in fury.

Hunter cupped her face in his hands; the rain sluicing over her cheeks and between his fingers. She turned her face and pressed a kiss into his palm, her heart beating so heavily it hurt. He made a sound of pain, of need, and drew her against him.

His mouth found hers, taking it quietly but with an edge of desperation that frightened her. Their tongues mated, their bodies melded. Through their soaked clothing, Aimee imagined she could feel the wild pump of Hunter's heart, that its beat met and blended with hers, creating one stronger, steadier beat. Creating one being where there had been two.

Dizzy, frightened, she stood on tiptoe and pressed her body more fully to his. He slid a hand to the back of her neck, curling his fingers possessively around her, burying his other hand in her wet hair.

The lights flickered, then went off. Blackness enveloped them. Oliver cried out for her.

For one excruciatingly brief moment, they stood frozen and clinging to one another. Then Hunter dropped his hands and stepped away from her. She felt his emotional wall drop back into place. She grieved—and rejoiced—at its coming. Now she was safe. And safety was the thing she wanted most...and least. "Hunter—" She lifted a hand, reaching out to him.

He took another step back. "Your son needs you," he murmured. "Go to him."

Turning away from her, he crossed the gallery and descended the stairs, stepping out into the storm. Aimee watched him until he was swallowed by the darkness.

Chapter Seven

From the back door, Aimee watched Oliver and Hunter play under the oak tree. Beside them, Tante Marie sat shucking oysters for the stew she had insisted on making for them tonight. What a pretty family picture they made, she thought. How happy they looked. How right together.

Aimee sighed and closed her eyes on the scene before her. In the days that had passed since her and Hunter's encounter on the rain-drenched gallery, she'd found it difficult to concentrate, to sleep, to eat. Time and again, she had caught her thoughts drifting to that night, and found herself analyzing every word they'd exchanged, every glance, every touch.

By some unspoken but mutual agreement, she and Hunter had hardly interacted at all since then. Oh, he'd been around. He'd worked with her father and played with Oliver, but he'd kept his distance from her.

She'd thanked the heavens for that unspoken agreement. For in her analyzing she'd come to understand something—Hunter was lonely; he needed her. Whether he realized it or not, that need had brought him here. And that frightened the hell out of her.

Aimee touched the screen lightly, trailing her fingers over its rough surface. She could rail against his determination to "do the right thing" by her; she could be infuriated by his guilt, his pity. But his loneliness, his pain, pulled at her, and she was powerless against it. She always had been.

She'd allowed Hunter to use her as an anesthetic before. That's what she'd been; she understood that now. Only now, she could use a painkiller, too. She was lonely. She hurt.

The two of them were a dangerous combination, indeed.

Aimee turned away from the scene before her. She had to think of Oliver, of his needs. Every day he grew more attached to Hunter. He'd never taken to anyone so quickly. Was her son so starved for male companionship? Even as the question filtered through her brain, she shook her head. That didn't make sense. He had lots of male relatives besides his *pépère*, all of whom took a great interest in him.

So why the case of hero worship? She drew her eyebrows together, concerned. And what did she do about it?

Outside, Oliver squealed with amusement, and Aimee smiled at the sound. Maybe she should just let it run its course. Hunter wouldn't be staying too much longer. His clinic had been calling more and more frequently; obviously, he was needed back in California. At this point she and Hunter were playing a waiting game. If the number of calls from the clinic was any indication, Hunter would be forced to concede soon.

Oliver laughed again, and Aimee looked back at him and Hunter. Her son would be sad when Hunter left, but he would get over it. He would have to. Hunter wouldn't give him any other choice.

Turning away from the screen once more, she headed back into the store. Once a month, she took a portfolio of photos around to the tourist gift shops and commercial galleries in the area. The photos depicted Cajun life, the bayous and swamps, and made good postcards and mementos. They were strictly a money-making venture for her, and they were the only photographs she took these days.

From behind the sales counter she collected her portfolio, purse and car keys. Carrying them to the front of the store, she waved goodbye to her father, who was on the phone.

She paused on the gallery to dig her sunglasses out of her purse. She slipped them on, then glanced up at the bright sky. Not even a cloud today to ease the relentless burn of the sun, she thought. Without air-conditioning, her car would be a furnace by noon.

She started down the steps, then stopped as her father called from inside.

"Aimee! Wait, *chère!*"

Biting back a sound of annoyance, Aimee went back up the steps. She dropped her portfolio and purse on one of the rocking chairs, and peeked back inside the store. "You need something, Papa?"

"I'm glad I caught you." He motioned her inside.

Drawing her eyebrows together, she stepped through the door, letting the screen slam shut behind her. "What's wrong? Has something happened to one of the family?"

"*Non.*" He held up his hands. "Everyone's fine. I need you to wheel me back to the house. I forgot my medication."

Annoyance at his request rippled over her. Guilty over it, she started toward him, ready to do his bidding. Hunter's words raced into her head, and she stopped. *"You're not helping him by coddling him, Aimee. If he's ever going to get better, he's going to have to start doing things for himself."*

"Chère?"

"Lose the guilt, Aimee. It's not doing either of you any good."

Aimee hesitated a moment more, struggling with that very thing. It was easy for Hunter to hand out advice, she thought. It wasn't *his* father in the wheelchair. It wasn't his father who had lost his sense of purpose, his reason for living. But still, Hunter's words had struck a chord of truth in her.

She wanted her father to get better. Didn't she?

Yes. She wanted that more than anything. Coming to a decision, Aimee took a deep breath and looked evenly at her father. "Why don't you wheel yourself over? I've got a full day of stops to make, and I need to get going."

Roubin stared at her, obviously surprised. Then he frowned. "But I need my medication. It will take you barely a minute."

Aimee hesitated again, torn between doing what she knew was right and feeling like she was betraying her father. She firmed her resolve and forced an easy smile. "You're perfectly capable of wheeling yourself across, Papa. You do it all the time." She checked her watch. "I should be back in plenty of time for supper."

"Why do you defy me?" Roubin demanded. "You know how difficult it is for me in this chair. It is easier for you to take me across. It is faster."

Guilt pulled at her. It *was* easier, *was* faster. He did have to fight his way across. But wasn't that the point?

Aimee cleared her throat. "I do too much for you. We both know it."

"You are being a good, dutiful daughter. That is all." He lifted a big hand to indicate the subject was closed. "Now, you will wheel me across."

"No, Papa, I won't." Aimee crossed to him, squatting down in front of the chair so their eyes would be on the same level. She smiled gently. "You're never going to get better if I keep doing everything for you. And I want you to get better."

Roubin clenched his hands into fists. "I'm never going to get better. This we both know."

"That's not what Dr. Landry says. Or Hunter." She stiffened her spine against the bitterness that tightened his features and covered his hands with her own. "I'm not going to coddle you any more. You're going to start doing some things for yourself."

"You would not talk to me so, if I weren't chained to this chair. You would have some respect!"

"I never had any respect. Remember?" She smiled, hoping to lighten his mood, wishing she could make him laugh the way Hunter could. "You used to wonder why *le bon Dieu* cursed you with such an ungrateful, mouthy daughter."

Roubin didn't reply. Instead, he withdrew his hands from hers and slowly, clumsily turned the chair away from her and started for the rear of the store. Aimee watched him go, tears stinging her eyes. He looked old and defeated. And so alone.

He'd lost everything. And now he felt she'd abandoned him as well.

Would it cost so much to do as he asked? she wondered. Wheeling him across, getting him his medications and a glass of water to take them with, was such a simple thing; it would take only minutes. Was it worth hurting him over?

Aimee curled her fingers into her palms, battling the urge to race after him. Wheeling him across now wasn't the issue, she reminded herself. The problem wasn't doing something for him once and awhile, but doing everything all the time. She didn't like to admit it, but Hunter was right. She would be a fool or completely self-destructive not to listen.

But even knowing it was for the best, denying her father hurt like hell.

Shaken, Aimee headed back out front to collect her things. She found Hunter there, leafing through her portfolio. She stopped, immediately angry at his presumption. How dare he look through her things without invitation? she thought, her heart beginning to thrum against the wall of her chest. How dare he?

She let the screen door slam noisily shut behind her. Hunter looked up, meeting her gaze. Instead of apology or embarrassment in his eyes, she saw disappointment. On the heels of what she'd just gone through with her father, the last thing she wanted or needed was a confrontation with Hunter. Working to control her anger, she stiffened her spine. "I don't believe I gave you permission to look through my portfolio."

"No wonder." He slipped one of the photos out of its sleeve and held it up. She'd taken it at a *fais-dodo;* it depicted a Cajun couple doing the two-step. "What is this, Aimee?"

She jerked her chin up, heat tinging her cheeks. "They sell well. The money is nice."

"You're too good to be doing this crap, technically excellent though it is."

"Excuse me," she said icily. "But I didn't ask for a critique. But then, I shouldn't be surprised. You're good at handing out unwanted advice." Telling herself she felt nothing but outrage, she marched across the gallery and held out her hand. "Butt out, Hunter."

He ignored her. "What happened to the artist who captured heart and soul with the eye of a camera? What happened to the visionary who believed in herself and her art, and was willing to go to the wall for it?"

Aimee narrowed her eyes, thinking of that girl and hating him for it. Hating that she felt like she had to explain, make excuses. "She needed to make a living.

She needed to support her son. Give me the photo, Hunter. I'm late."

"Isn't the truth more that she was frightened away by a few critics' disparaging remarks? Isn't the truth more that she let a bunch of creeps who could only dream of having a fraction of her talent scare her away?"

A trembling started deep inside her and spread, until even her fingertips shook. She told herself she was angry. Furious. She knew it was hurt, and disappointment in herself, that made her shake.

"You have no idea," she said softly, cursing the tremor in her voice, "what I felt back then. Or why I ran. You were too wrapped up in your own misery to understand mine. You still are."

Aimee grabbed for the photo just as Hunter pulled his hand back. The photo ripped down the center, the smiling, dancing couple forever torn asunder. Aimee gazed at the mutilated image, making a sound of distress. And surprise. She lifted her gaze to meet Hunter's. He, too, stared at the ripped photo, his expression startled.

He met her eyes. "Aimee...damn. I'm sorry. I didn't mean..."

He took a step toward her, hand out in a apology. She took a step back, lifting her chin, battling for control, for nonchalance. It took everything she had, but she managed both. "Don't worry about it. I have six more just like it." She relaxed her fingers, and her half of the torn photo fluttered to the gallery floor. Without glancing at it again, she collected her things and walked away.

Hunter watched her go, not looking away until her car had disappeared from sight. Then he lowered his gaze to the photo, its ragged, ripped edge mocking him. What had he hoped to accomplish by badgering her? he wondered, gazing at the image. What did he hope to accomplish by being here? He frowned. Did he think he could fix Aimee's life? Was that why he was here? Hell, he couldn't even fix his own.

He stooped and picked up the piece of the photograph she'd dropped. Uncanny how the photo had ripped directly down its center, forever rending the man and woman from each other's arms.

His frown deepening, Hunter fitted the two halves of the photo together. No matter how carefully he tried to piece one half to the other, the rip still showed.

It couldn't be fixed.

It would never be whole or without flaw again.

Hunter looked at his hands. A doctor's hands. Hands used to heal. Hands adroit enough, sensitive enough, to locate a person's pain simply through the sense of touch. But he hadn't helped Aimee. In fact, he'd complicated her life. Made her unhappier.

Maybe he should go, he thought, drawing his eyebrows together. He could stay in contact with Aimee and who knew, he might someday be able to convince her to take support for Oliver. Someday she might realize she needed it.

From the side of the house, he heard Oliver's laughter and his throat tightened. He'd grown accustomed to the boy's presence. To the sound of his laughter, to his childish enthusiasm and wide-eyed curiosity. He would miss that, Hunter realized. He would miss it a lot.

A moment later the boy barreled into view, Tante Marie lumbering behind. *"Loup garou!"* Oliver cried. "Help!"

Marie growled and bared her teeth, and Hunter laughed at the sight. The *loup garou* was the Cajun werewolf and Oliver's favorite monster. And no wonder, Hunter thought, amused. Both his grandfather and aunt filled his head with tales of the beast.

Marie growled again, gaining on the boy; Oliver squealed in delighted terror. Laughing, Hunter squatted down and held out his arms. "Here, Oliver. I'll protect you."

A second later Oliver was in his arms, pressed against his chest, clinging to him. Hunter stood, wrapping himself tightly around the child. Oliver's small body trembled with manufactured fear and with laughter; he was warm and smelled like a boy who had been playing hard.

Hunter breathed deeply. How many times had he held Pete like this? A hundred? A thousand? Hunter squeezed his eyes shut, the memories filling his head— of Pete crying out in the night, of going to him, of holding and rocking him.

"Daddy has you, Pete. Don't worry, baby. Daddy won't let anything hurt you. Not ever."

Pete had believed him. Had trusted him. But Hunter hadn't protected his baby, hadn't been there when the monster had come to call. Had Pete thought of that in his final minutes? Had his last thought been that his daddy had betrayed him?

Anguish hit Hunter in a debilitating wave. With the anguish came the smell of the fire, the sickening scent of death. The image of Pete in the morgue.

"Where are you, Daddy? I'm scared. I need you."

"Daddy's here. I'll never let anything happen to you, Pete. Not ever."

Pain knotted in Hunter's chest, and he fought to hold back the cry of pain. He held Oliver tighter, as if to let go of him would be to let go of life.

Dear God. Why not me instead? Why not me—

Oliver leaned back in Hunter's arms. "Get you now," he said, curving his hands into claws and growling in his imitation of the werewolf. "Monster coming!"

Hunter stared blankly at the boy, his memories mixing with Oliver's words. One second became ten; Hunter's head began to clear.

"Get you now," the boy said again. "Better run."

Hunter blinked. The nightmare image of Pete shifted, then evaporated; he suddenly saw Oliver's face before his own. Clearly and as if for the first time. He's so beautiful, Hunter thought, a place deep inside him opening. So special and bright.

The tightness in his chest eased, then filled with something warm and light. Hunter's mouth lifted into a smile. The smile led to a laugh, one that sprang from the very center of his being.

Oliver frowned. "No laugh! Monster!" He growled again. *"Loup garou!"*

Hunter laughed again, unable to hold it back. It pressed against his insides, occupying the same space the pain had only moments before, shouting to be released. Hunter threw his head back and laughed up at the heavens, laughing until his eyes ran and his sides ached.

"Wind again," Oliver demanded, watching the music box's belle come slowly to a stop. He looked up at Hunter, sitting on the porch step beside him. "I like it. Pretty."

Hunter smiled and did as the child asked, even though he'd rewound the box a half dozen times already. As the belle inside the dome began once again to circle the base, Oliver giggled.

A week had passed since the afternoon he'd held Oliver and laughed until he cried. In those moments, something had happened to him. Something warm. Something bright.

He didn't know if what he'd felt had been some sort of miracle or only a brief respite from the cold. But whichever, the last seven days had been the best, the most relaxed, since he'd lost Ginny and Pete. Hunter smiled. In fact, he'd felt, ridiculously, as if anything were possible. Even happy endings.

Hunter touched Oliver's silky hair, gently stroking for a moment. He'd enjoyed Oliver's company. Thoroughly. Without nightmarish remembrances of Pete. Without the guilt and regrets that had torn at him before.

He liked the boy. He was bright and gentle and kind. He wasn't as rugged and outgoing as Pete had been, but then Pete hadn't been as thoughtful or curious. As Aimee had said to him weeks before, they were two very different children and shouldn't be compared.

Aimee called out from the wheelchair path, and both he and Oliver looked up. She and Roubin were headed toward them, Roubin with a large picnic basket on his lap. Oliver had been burbling about this upcoming picnic for several days now, and beside him the child began to bounce with excitement.

"I better take this inside, Tiger," Hunter said, plucking the music box from Oliver's hands. "Be right back."

He took the box back to his room, returning to the porch just as Aimee and Roubin had reached it.

"Ready to go?" Aimee asked Oliver, grinning as if she already knew the answer.

"Yippee!" Oliver jumped up. "Going to fish," he announced proudly, looking back at Hunter. "Pépère promised."

Roubin chuckled. "Today, maybe you will catch a fish big enough for our dinner."

"This big," Oliver said, holding his arms out.

"You catch a fish that size, *petit-fils,* and the newspaper, she will come and do a story about you."

Oliver beamed, obviously liking the idea.

Hunter sauntered forward, eyeing the basket on Roubin's lap, not too proud to try to angle an invitation to the party. "Judging by the size of that basket, you must have enough to feed an army."

"Not an army," Aimee said coolly. "Just us."

Hunter slipped his hands into his pockets and cocked his head. "I don't believe I've been on a picnic...since we were together in California."

Hunter watched as a delicious shade of rose eased over Aimee's cheeks. They'd picnicked together more than once when they'd lived together. And made love with the warm breeze against their naked backs. He could tell by her blush that she, too, remembered.

"Mmm." He grinned. "Nothing's better than eating cold fried chicken under a big, shady tree on a warm spring day." They'd eaten chicken on those picnics in the past. And licked each other's fingers clean.

Her color heightened more. "Too bad. We're having sandwiches."

"Like I said," Hunter said smoothly, "nothing's better than eating sandwiches—"

"Come on, *chère,*" Roubin interrupted, a twinkle in his eye, "we cannot leave our guest with nothing to eat. How would it look?"

"Can he come, Maman?" Oliver begged, clapping his hands together. "Please!"

Hunter fought back a grin and gazed at her with what he hoped were irresistible, puppy dog eyes.

With a shake of her head and a quick grin, she gave in. "All right, you can come. But I warn you all..." She wagged a finger at them. "...if anybody eats more than two sandwiches, somebody will go hungry. And I promise you, it won't be me."

The amused and teasing atmosphere prevailed, setting the tone for the entire outing. Even the weather cooperated by providing a cloudless blue sky, unusually low humidity and deliciously moderate temperature.

After consuming every sandwich—and playfully fighting over the last—Roubin took Oliver down to the bayou's edge to fish. Hunter stayed behind with

Aimee, sprawled beside her on the blanket, and she didn't know whether to rejoice or wail over that fact.

She couldn't resist him when he was being so attentive and charming. But then, she wasn't sure she wanted to. She drew in a deep, easy breath. For the time being, she would let the moment—and the future—take care of itself.

Leaning back on her elbows, she smiled sleepily as she watched her father show Oliver how to cast. The change in her father over the past week was nothing short of remarkable. He was smiling and laughing. He seemed to be enjoying life again, even if only a bit.

She tipped her head, studying her father's expression. Now, his face was the picture of patience. And contentment.

Contentment, she thought, sighing and closing her eyes. The way she felt at this moment. Contented and sleepy and ready for whatever life threw her.

"Penny for your thoughts."

Aimee opened her eyes and looked at Hunter. His gaze was as blue as the spring sky above. And today, for this moment anyway, just as cloudless.

"You were right about Papa," she said simply. "He's doing well. Better than I've seen him since his illness."

Hunter looked at the older man, then back at her, frowning. "I was too hard on you. I didn't mean to be. I'm sorry."

"Don't apologize. You were right. I needed the proverbial kick in the rear." She smiled. "Not that I didn't despise you for it at the time."

"I despised myself for it. I couldn't seem to..." He shook his head and looked away. "Forget it."

"No, Hunter. What?"

From beyond the edge of the blanket, Hunter plucked a long blade of grass. He twirled it in his fingers for a moment before looking her fully in the face once more. "That night, I looked at you, and all I could think about was you in my arms. In my bed. But I knew those were the last places you wanted or needed to be."

He tossed the velvety blade of grass aside. "I was hard on you because I couldn't be soft. Couldn't be gentle. Not without taking you in my arms. Again."

Aimee glanced uncomfortably away. What could she say to that? How could she respond? Tell him that his arms, his bed, was where she wanted to be, even though she knew it was impossible? Should she thank him for saving her when she would rather curse him for it?

She sat up and curled her legs protectively under her. "Congratulations, Doc," she quipped. "The surgery was a success."

For one long moment, he didn't move, didn't even seem to breathe. Then he caught her hand, forcing her to meet his eyes once more. "Helping your father wasn't about being a doctor."

The breath lodged in her throat, and she wetted her suddenly parched lips. "No?"

"No." He ran his fingers over hers, exploring, exciting. "It was about caring. For you. For your father. It was about wanting you to be happy."

"Oh," she murmured, not knowing what else to say but simultaneously cursing the inane little word.

"Damn, you're beautiful."

Aimee lifted her gaze, surprised at the compliment, feeling color flood her cheeks. "What brought that on?"

"Looking at you."

"Oh," she said again, and again called herself a fool. He dragged his thumb across the translucent skin of her wrist; her pulse scrambled in response.

Could he feel the wild beat of her heart? she wondered, a catch in her chest. Could he feel her need, her confusion?

"Aimee?" he murmured, his voice thick.

"I should check on Oliver," she said quickly, starting to rise.

Hunter tightened his fingers, tumbling her back down to the blanket beside him. "He's fine. He's having fun with his grandfather."

In the branches above, a bird burst into song. The breeze stirred the leaves, bringing with it the sweet scent of flowers. The sun warmed; the bayou lapped gently against the bank.

Even Mother Nature was conspiring against her, Aimee thought, her muscles loosening, her pulse slowing. And how could she fight Mother Nature?

She couldn't. Simple as that. With a shake of her head, Aimee relaxed against the blanket once again, letting the beauty of the day surround her, the magic of the moment. The magic of being with Hunter.

"Have you missed . . . California?" he asked, after a moment.

Aimee paused, then nodded. "Yes." She drew in a deep breath, then released it. "I miss the pace. I miss all the things there were to do there. The galleries and museums, the shows. I miss being able to talk to people who think as I do."

But most of all, she thought, meeting his eyes, I miss loving you . . . miss being with you.

Hunter plucked another blade of grass from the ground beside them. Again, he toyed with it. "And your photography? Do you miss it?"

Her chest tightened. "Of course."

"Then why did you give it up? Why did you go?"

"How can you ask?" she whispered, emotion choking the words. "I did what I had to. To survive. I had no friends, a part-time job that paid minimum wage, and I was pregnant."

"I would have helped you."

"I didn't want that. I still . . . don't."

Hunter caught her hand and brought it to his mouth, pressing a gentle kiss in her palm. Then turning it over, he laid the blade of grass in her palm and curled her fingers around it. "I know."

Aimee stared at her closed hand, then brought her gaze back up to his. She didn't know what that gesture signified, she only knew how it made her feel. Connected to him in an elemental way. Powerless yet safe. Terrified.

Clutching the blade of grass, she said, "Every one of my dreams blew up in my face at once, Hunter. My dream of you loving me, of us living happily ever after. My dream of being a famous artist. I was a fool. A silly, naive girl who thought she could make things happen just by wanting them to."

She opened her hand and gazed at the slim sliver of green. "I needed you desperately. You weren't there for me. Just as you always told me you wouldn't be. But you see, like a willful and stubborn child, I had believed only what I wanted to. Then when everything came crashing in on me, I saw. In a sort of epiphany of pain, I finally saw the truth about us.

"I had no one. When my show bombed, my friends deserted me." She drew in a deep, ragged breath. "So I went home. And found my father a changed man. Bitter and angry. I hadn't even known he was sick." She met Hunter's eyes. "He almost died, but I wasn't here for him. I was off chasing rainbows."

"He didn't contact you, Aimee. If he had, you would have gone to his side. You know you would have."

"But don't you see? He'd told me I would be dead to him until I came home. He'd meant it." Her eyes filled. "I hadn't believed him. Just as I hadn't believed you when you told me you would never love me. I was wrong about everything."

Hunter touched her cheek with the tips of his fingers. "I'm sorry I wasn't there for you."

"I know you are."

"And I wish I could . . . change that time."

She leaned her head into his caress. "You can't."

"No."

Silence fell between them. Aimee breathed deeply, sobered by their talk but not sad. She looked up at the crystalline sky, then back at Hunter and smiled. "I'm not completely unhappy, you know. I love the bayou. Her sounds and scents. Her mysteries. I grew up here, and she feels like home. I love my family, my people. Oliver is happy. He has family here, a connection that goes beyond me to who he is and what he will always be a part of. That's important.''

As if cued, Oliver squealed and called for her. She looked up to see him holding up his fishing line, the fish on its end fighting for its life, flashing silver in the sunlight. She gave her son a thumbs-up sign and shouted her congratulations. In the next moment her father showed Oliver how to get the fish off the hook without damaging its mouth, then together they threw it back. She smiled. If her father had anything to say about it, her son would be a very good fisherman.

She turned back to Hunter to find his blue gaze intently upon her. Something in his expression had her catching her breath. ''What?''

''The only warmth I've known since Ginny and Pete died has been with you.'' He caught her hand once more. ''You thought you weren't important to me. That you didn't make a difference in my life. You did. I don't know if I would have made it through that time without you.''

She swallowed past the lump in her throat, unsure what to say, what to do. As if reading her thoughts, he shook his head and curled his fingers tightly around hers, indicating that she should just let him talk.

''I was out of town when...it happened,'' he began, clutching her fingers even tighter. ''At a medical convention. Pete wanted to come with me. He begged me to let him. But, I was giving a paper, an important one, and I was nervous. I didn't want the...distraction.''

Hunter fell silent, and Aimee saw his struggle for control. Saw how much it hurt him to verbalize this part of his past. Aching for him, she returned the pressure of his fingers.

"I told him everything would be fine," he continued, his voice raspy. "I'd be home in four days, I'd bring him something special. I didn't get the chance. Two nights later, in the middle of . . . the night . . ."

He didn't finish the sentence. He didn't have to. Aimee knew what had happened. Their pricey Laguna Beach home had caught fire; Ginny and Pete had not escaped in time.

"I've died a million guilty deaths since then," Hunter whispered. "If only I'd brought them with me. If only I'd listened to him. Maybe he knew, on some instinctive level, that something terrible was going to happen. You know, like people who at the last minute decide not to board a plane that crashes later. But he was a child, he couldn't control . . . he only had me to turn to . . . to take care of him. And I . . . let him down. I let them both down."

"Oh Hunter . . ." Aimee brought his hand to her face, and laid her cheek against it. "The truth is that he loved his daddy and wanted to be with him. Don't second-guess like that. Don't speculate. It'll kill you."

"And would that be so bad?"

Her tears brimmed and spilled over, rolling slowly down her cheeks. "I think so," she whispered. "I think it would be terrible."

Hunter sucked in a deep, steadying breath. "I didn't know, Aimee. Until they were gone . . . I just . . . didn't know."

She squeezed his fingers even tighter, her own numb from the pressure. "What?" she asked softly. "What didn't you know?"

"That they were the only things that were important."

Her breath caught. Reaching up, she cupped his face in her palms. She gazed into his eyes, glassy with emotion. One moment became two became a dozen. Slowly, she drew his head down to hers. Their lips met. She brushed her mouth against his gently and with infinite care, telling him without words everything she felt for him. Holding nothing back.

He shuddered and curved his arms around her back. For long moments, he held her tightly. Then he eased away and gazed at her, searching her expression, his own haunted. Not by the memories of their time together, their failed love affair. But by the ghosts of his wife and child.

It had always been this way between them.

Without another word, Hunter stood and walked off. He headed away from the bayou and the three of them, and as much as it hurt to let him go, Aimee knew he needed to be alone.

She stared after him, her heart in her throat. Dear Lord, she loved him still. After everything, despite his ghosts, she still loved him.

How big a fool could she be?

A big one, she realized, clasping her shaking hands in her lap. Tears welled in her eyes. She would walk through fire for him. She would sacrifice her needs— for love and commitment, for emotional devotion—to be with him.

If she had only herself to think of.

She didn't. She turned her gaze to her son, his head bent in concentration as his grandfather baited his hook. She had Oliver to think of. He deserved a real family. With a father and mother who loved each other without reservation, without ghosts. And he deserved a father who would love him more than anything in the world.

The way Hunter had loved Pete.

Aimee lowered her eyes. On the blanket by her knee lay the blade of grass Hunter had handed her. Drawing her eyebrows together, she picked it up. Hunter had opened up to her more than he ever had before. He had told her how much he'd appreciated her back then, told her she'd been important to him.

But he hadn't said a word about love. Hadn't said a word about the future. And he never would. What Hunter had given her today was the most he ever would. Aimee closed her fingers over the piece of grass. Hunter had no more to offer her now than he had three and a half years ago.

Only now, she had a lot more—and less—to lose.

She opened her fist, and the blade of green dropped to the blanket. The time had come to get on with her life. After mass last Sunday, Roberto had cornered her and asked her to this week's *fais-dodo.* She'd refused.

Why? she wondered, gazing once more at her son. What was she waiting for? For Hunter to ask her?

She had to get on with her life, she thought again. She had to fall out of love with Hunter. Oliver deserved a real family. He deserved a father. He would never have either if she didn't do something about it.

If she didn't face reality and stop clinging to her love for a man who could never love her back. A man who would never give her a happy-ever-after.

She would call Roberto and accept his invitation. And start living again. Before it was too late. For her. For Oliver.

Tears stinging her eyes, Aimee reached for the bit of grass, only to find it had been carried away by the breeze.

Chapter Eight

"*You're going to the fais-dodo?*" Aimee asked, looking at her father in surprise. He hadn't been to a *fais-dodo* since his illness. In fact, she hadn't been able to budge him from the property for anything but doctor appointments and the most special family functions. "Tonight?"

"*Oui,*" her father announced, handing her his empty gumbo bowl. "We are all going."

Aimee slid her gaze to Hunter. He leaned back in his chair and smiled at her. The proverbial Cheshire cat. "You knew about this?"

Hunter shrugged. "Roubin mentioned it. This morning."

Aimee glanced back at her father. "It would have been nice if he'd mentioned it to *me.*"

"*Pardon, chère.* You were busy."

She cleared away the remaining gumbo bowls, annoyed to see that her hands shook. When she had agreed to accompany Roberto to the *fais-dodo,* she hadn't anticipated having to announce it this way. What *had* she anticipated? she wondered. Slinking out of the house like a criminal?

Aimee squared her shoulders. Why should announcing her plans in front of Hunter bother her? She had nothing to hide from him or anyone else.

She carried the bowls to the sink. "Well, you should have interrupted me, Papa, because now it's impossible."

"Not to worry," he said, his eyes alight with mischief. "I have made arrangements for my *petit-fils.* Clementine, she has offered to watch him. With her broken toe, she cannot dance." Aimee opened her mouth, and he held up a hand to stop any arguments. "It is all set. And Oliver, he is excited about spending the night with his cousins."

Aimee looked down the hall to Oliver's room. She could hear him playing with his toys. She shook her head in disbelief. Oliver hadn't said a word about his cousins. When had her son learned to keep secrets from her?

She turned back to Roubin, narrowing her eyes. Her father, the same man who'd had to be badgered into wheeling himself across the yard just over a week ago, had planned all this? By himself? Even making arrangements for Oliver? Impossible. Unbelievable.

Unless he was up to something.

She placed her fists on her hips. "Okay, Papa, spill it."

"What do you mean, *chère?*"

His innocence was as false as a Yankee's attempt at *étouffée.* He all but batted his eyelashes at her. "I mean, what's going on?"

"You are so suspicious." He brought his coffee mug to his lips, looking irritated. "We are going to the dance. You are young. You should be having fun. You should be dancing. I thought you would be happy that I did something for myself."

As she opened her mouth to apologize, he gave himself away. He glanced at Hunter from the corners of his eyes, all but giggling, and the truth hit her like a sack of oysters. Her father was matchmaking.

She let out her breath in an annoyed huff. She shouldn't be surprised. Her father had made it clear from the beginning that he expected Hunter to do the right thing by her. That he expected her to do the right thing by Oliver. And now, judging by the amount of time he was spending with Hunter, her father's desire to get them together had surpassed "doing the right thing." Now, he liked Hunter and saw that Oliver did, too.

The old goat, she thought, fuming. He'd decided to give her and Hunter a little push in the right direction. Once again, he'd decided that he knew what was best for her. Wouldn't he be surprised when she told him Roberto had already invited her to the *fais-dodo,* and that she'd accepted.

She went back to the table for the bread plates and silverware. "Well, you still should have checked with me, Papa. I already have a date for the dance."

"A date?" Roubin and Hunter repeated simultaneously.

"A date," Aimee murmured, careful not to look at Hunter, though unsure what she hoped, or dreaded, seeing in his expression. Or, what she feared he would see in hers. "With Roberto."

"Roberto? *Non,* Aimee." Roubin shook his head. "His blood, it is no good."

"Papa—"

"*Bon Dieu!* His cousin, Placide, he is a drunk. His sister runs as wild as the muskrat in the swamp. And his *maman . . .*" Roubin shook his head again and held his arms wide apart, "...she is *très grasse.* You know these things, *chère.*"

Aimee took a deep breath, daring a peek at Hunter. He sat absolutely still, his face a mask of indifference. Annoyed, she turned back to her father. "Roberto's a nice man, Papa. A good man. It's time I started dating again, and Roberto wants to date me."

"*Non.* I do not like this."

"Sorry to hear that, but I'm a grown-up and can make my own decisions. I'm going." She plucked his half-full coffee cup from his hands, then grabbed Hunter's. "Discussion's over, Papa. If you'll both excuse me, I need to get this place cleaned up so I can get ready for my date."

Without waiting for a response, she turned back to the sink and began to fill it with water. Behind her, her father muttered in French about ungrateful daughters and bad blood as he wheeled himself out of the kitchen. Aimee waited a moment, listening, expecting to hear Hunter push his chair away from the table and follow her father. Instead, she felt his gaze on her back.

He didn't speak. Seemed not to even move. She heard no rustle of clothes, no creak of furniture or flooring.

The silence was deafening.

Swearing to herself, she slid the bowls into the water, being deliberately noisy, wanting to drown out the sound of his silence.

Instead, his silence became louder. His scrutiny more intense. She swore again, this time aloud. She did not feel guilty, she told herself. She did not feel like a liar or a fraud. She was doing what she had to. What was right—for her, for Oliver.

Then why was she acting guilty? Why was she acting like she had something to hide?

She wasn't, she told herself, scrubbing one bowl, then another. She didn't wish to talk to him right now. That was all. She didn't want a scene. If he would just stop staring at her, everything would be fine.

He didn't cooperate. As usual.

With a sound of impatience, Aimee slammed off the water and spun around to face him. As she'd known he would be, he was staring at her.

"What?" she asked.

He lifted his eyebrows. "I didn't say anything."

"You didn't have to." She grabbed the dish towel and dried her hands with quick, jerky motions. "Let's not play games, Hunter. You have something on your mind. Spit it out."

"All right." He stood and crossed to her, stopping directly in front of her. She inched her chin up, setting her jaw stubbornly. "Earlier, you asked your father what he was doing. I'm wondering the same thing about you." With his index finger he brushed a soap bubble from her cheek. "Want to clue me in, Slick?"

She cocked up her chin another notch. "I'm doing the dishes."

"That's not what I mean. And you know it. I'm talking about Roberto and your . . . date."

"What's so difficult to understand?" She folded her arms across her chest. "Unattached female goes dancing with unattached male. The scenario is an old one. Surely you've heard of it?"

"Now who's playing games?"

Heat stung her cheeks. He was right, and she was above playing games. At least, she liked to think she was. She turned back to the sink and plunged her hands into the warm, soapy water. What *was* she doing?

And worse, what was she hoping?

End this now, she thought. Do it this moment and cleanly, before something happened that she would regret forever. Something that would complicate this already impossible situation.

Taking a deep breath, Aimee looked him fully in the face without wavering. "It's time for you to go home, Hunter. I want you to go. People here are starting to hope for things that will never happen."

For several seconds, Hunter searched her gaze. Then he took a step closer, stopping so close he obliterated her view of everything but him. "What people, Aimee?"

Me, she admitted silently, dying a little inside as she did. She loved him, and her heart was already broken.

"Oliver," she said instead, quietly. "Papa." She turned back to the dishes. "It's going to hurt them when you leave, and the longer you stay, the more it will hurt."

"And when are you going to leave, Aimee?"

Under the cover of the sudsy water, she clenched her hands into fists. It hurt to have him refer to her future, a future that didn't include him. She thought of Roberto and of opportunities. "I'm not. This is my home."

"You don't belong here. When are you going to admit that? You did once."

"No, Hunter. It's you who doesn't belong. Go back to La La Land. Leave us alone."

She turned back to the dishes, shutting him out. He caught her arm, forcing her to face him. "The other day you told me you weren't 'completely unhappy.' Come on, Aimee. You belong here no more than I do. When are you going to stop hiding and start living again?"

His words would be laughable if they weren't so tragic. He was right—and wrong—and neither made a damn bit of difference. So she held on to her anger, her frustration, throwing both back at him.

"I do belong, Hunter. I intend to stay." She put a hand on his chest, curling her wet, soapy fingers into the soft cotton of his pullover. "I'm going to marry a good Cajun, raise Oliver and have more babies. Right here in La Fin. I'm going to be happy."

She tightened her fingers, wanting to wound him as he'd wounded her. "And while I'm being happy, Hunter, what are you going to be? Alone?"

A muscle worked in his jaw. "If that's true, Aimee, why have you waited so long? Where is your 'good Cajun'?"

Aimee gazed up at him, water from her hands dripping down her arms, puddling at her feet. They both knew why there was no man in her life; she would die before admitting it out loud.

She jerked her arm from his grasp. "That may be him calling for me at eight," she said softly. "So, if you'll excuse me, I need to get ready."

Without waiting for a reply, she turned and walked away, leaving Hunter and the unfinished dishes behind.

Hunter stood on Aimee's front gallery, the blood thrumming in his head, frustration and jealousy churning inside him. Behind him, the bayou slept. Before him, the road curved empty and black. Mocking him.

Where the hell was she?

Roubin had arrived home hours ago. It had been nearly that long since the last car had passed the store. Hunter knocked his fist against one of the gallery's cypress columns. It was after midnight; what could they be doing?

A picture of exactly what they might be doing filled his head, and Hunter's jaw tightened. Why had he let her go? He should have punched the other guy silly, then dragged her off.

Great technique, Hunter thought, reaching for his can of beer. That really would have impressed her.

Tipping his head back Hunter took a long swallow of the brew, enjoying its almost bitter bite. Roberto had called for Aimee precisely at eight. Dark in the way of the Cajuns who were descended from French and Spanish blood, Roberto was handsome. Too handsome. Vital and fit in the way of a man who worked with his hands and back for a living.

Hunter had expected someone different, someone less good-looking. Less confident with women. Aimee had called the man nice, for heaven's sake. Who would have expected Don Juan from that description?

Swearing again, Hunter began to pace. Aimee had looked gorgeous. Unbelievably sexy. She'd exchanged her usual blue jeans or cutoffs for a red-and-white striped halter dress in a crisp cotton. The fabric had hugged her breasts, and revealed her smooth shoulders and an alarming expanse of her back. The image of Roberto's hands on Aimee's bare skin filled his head, and Hunter stopped pacing. With his mind's eye he saw the other man's hands moving slowly across her shoulders, easing down her spine. He imagined the man pressing his mouth to the side of her throat, to the curve of a shoulder.

Hunter flexed his fingers, ready to commit murder. If that dark-haired Lothario so much as touched her, Hunter would have his head.

Headlights sliced across the darkness. Hunter turned toward the road, adrenaline pumping through him. The car came into view but didn't slow, didn't turn into the drive. It passed the store, leaving only darkness behind.

Hunter drew in a deep breath, the air heavy with jasmine. The scent teased him. Taunted him. Hunter brought the beer to his lips once more. He wanted to shout, wanted to hit something. He wanted to kiss Aimee until she came to her senses.

And realized what? Aimee had been right. He didn't belong here; he had nothing to offer her. The time had come for him to go home.

But none of that meant a damn right now. He couldn't have Aimee with another man. He didn't have a clue what he was going to do about it, how he was going to stop her, he only knew he had to.

With a last look at the dark road, Hunter went in search of another beer.

Aimee folded her hands in her lap and looked sightlessly out the car window. Hunter had never shown up at the *fais-dodo*. She'd watched for him, waited for him, the breath of expectation hot and tight in her chest.

She'd seen her father. He'd made quite a commotion when he'd wheeled into the hall. Friends and neighbors, people from all over the parish who had known him all his life, rushed to express their happiness at seeing him out and to wish him well. It had brought tears to her eyes, and she had seen that he, too, had been moved. His eyes had been bright, his hands shaky.

Of course, he'd only glared at her and Roberto. Particularly Roberto. Aimee shook her head, breathing a sigh of relief as Roberto turned into her driveway. When her father got an idea in his head, it was there to stay. Roberto didn't have a chance with him.

Or with her. She glanced at him from the corner of her eyes. It was too bad. Roberto was sweet. And attentive. He deserved more than a woman who was with him only in the hopes of falling out of love with another man; he deserved better than a woman who desired him only to make another jealous.

There, she thought, her chest tightening. She'd admitted it. A part of the reason she'd said yes to Roberto's invitation had been in the hope that she would make Hunter jealous. In the hope that her dating would force him to make . . . a move. To realize some things.

If there was even anything for him to realize.

Hysterical laughter bubbled to her lips. How much lower could she sink? To have used another man that way was immature, sophomoric. She twisted her fingers together. It was despicable.

"Penny for your thoughts," Roberto murmured, pulling the car to a stop beside her house. He cut off the engine and headlights.

Hunter had said those same words to her only days before. The day she'd realized that nothing had changed, that she still loved Hunter to the exclusion of everything, even good sense.

The memory brought an ache and she lowered her eyes. "You'd be wasting your money," she said, hearing the wistfulness in her own voice and wondering if Roberto did, too.

"I do not think so." Turning toward her, Roberto reached across the seat and covered her hands with one of his own. "I had a good time tonight."

"I did, too."

He squeezed her hands. "What is wrong, *chère?* I have known you since you were a *petite-fille,* and tonight you were not yourself."

She looked down at their hands, then up at him, her eyes bright with tears. "It's complicated. I . . . there's someone else."

"Your 'old friend' from California?"

She flushed. "How did you know?"

He smiled sadly and withdrew his hand. "I have eyes."

"I'm sorry."

"Don't be. It is I who is sorry. If it doesn't work out, call me. I will be here."

"Thank you."

Roberto got out of the car and came around to open the door for her. She alighted from the vehicle and together they walked toward the house.

"You don't have to see me up," she said as they stopped at the base of the gallery steps. Her father had left a light burning inside, its gentle glow illuminated the steps and door.

Roberto leaned toward her and lightly brushed his mouth against hers. "Good night, *chère.*"

Her heart heavy, Aimee watched as he climbed back into his car and drove off. When his taillights had disappeared from view, she sighed and started up the steps. Why couldn't she love him? Life would be so much simpler. So much easier.

"Hello, Aimee."

She caught her breath in surprise and swung toward the darkest edge of the gallery. Hunter stood by the porch swing, a can of Dixie beer in his hand. "You startled me."

"Evidently." He lifted the can to his lips, took a long swallow, then set the can on the swing. "How was your...date?"

Her hackles rose at the sarcasm in his voice. "It was great," she said. "Fabulous."

"I could tell by your good-night kiss."

She told herself to say good-night and go inside. She folded her arms across her chest and inched her chin up instead. "Meaning?"

"Meaning, you could hardly stand to have him touch you."

She caught her breath as anger, white-hot, shot through her. How dare he spy on her? How dare he stand there and smugly tell her what she felt? She curled her hands into fists, the urge to slap him charging through her.

"I don't think much of your assessment of my feelings," she murmured. "In fact, I don't think you could see how I felt if I was wearing a sign."

Hunter stepped out of the shadows and into the soft circle of light that tumbled from the window. In his eyes she saw violence, tightly leashed. The same anger, she knew, was mirrored in her own eyes.

"Did he touch you?"

"Waiting up for me, Hunter? Like a worried father?" She lifted her eyebrows, the cool gesture the antithesis of the emotion churning inside her. "Or a jealous lover?"

"Don't push me, Aimee." He took a step toward her. "I asked you a question."

"Mr. Cool might lose it. That would be a first." She angled her head back, knowing she was playing with fire but not giving a damn. "I'm so scared."

He moved closer, stopping so close she had tip her head back to meet his eyes. Heat blazed in them. "Did he touch you?" he asked again.

"I don't kiss and tell."

"And I warned you not to push me." He cupped her face, his fingers biting into her flesh. "Did he?"

"Go home," she whispered, bringing her hands to his chest. "You've no claim on me. No right to be jealous." In a mockery of her own words, she clenched her fingers into the soft weave of his shirt, anchoring herself to him. Beneath her palm, his heart thundered. "I want you to leave me and Oliver alone."

Hunter laughed, the sound hard. "Liar. When I touch you, your body gives you away. The last thing you want is for me to leave you alone." He pressed closer, cementing their bodies. "What you did tonight... don't do it again. You belong to me, Aimee."

"I don't." She tried to shake her head in denial, but his hands held her captive. "I want to marry Roberto or someone like him, someone who's alive. Someone who can feel something besides pain."

"You're mine," he repeated firmly, moving his hands to her hair, wrapping his fingers in the heavy, dark strands.

"No." She pushed against his chest, hating him for his words, hating herself because they were true. Furious, she met his eyes. "I stopped feeling anything for you long ago, Hunter. I stopped wanting you, stopped loving you."

"Mistake, Aimee," he muttered. "Big...big mistake."

A moment later, his mouth crashed down on hers, capturing her denials, taking her by surprise. If not for his hands in her hair, the force of his kiss would have sent her stumbling backward.

But she didn't stumble, didn't retreat. She met his force with her own, curving her fingers around his shoulders, digging at him with her nails. Punishing him because he hadn't left the past alone, because she still loved him. And punishing him because loving him was a dead-end street.

He tore his mouth from hers, his breath coming in short gasps. He loosened his fingers, caressing now instead of bruising. "If you had simply told me to leave, I would have. But to tell me you feel nothing for me..." He spanned her neck with his hands, softly stroking her throbbing pulse points. "We both know that's a lie."

She let out a shuddering breath. "I don't want it to be."

"I know. I don't either." He inched her backward, out of the circle of light, until her back pressed against the side of the house. The shadows and the scent of the jasmine, thick and ripe, enfolded them. "But, heaven help me, I want you."

He flattened himself against her. The cypress siding bit into her back, her shoulder blades. He pressed his mouth to her neck, tasting. A soft sigh of pleasure slipped from her lips, mingling with the sultry sounds of the night. Nipping, exploring, he trailed his mouth across her collarbone, to the roundness of her shoulder. He nudged aside the strap of her dress to tease the vulnerable beginning of a breast. She curved her hands around his shoulders and arched against him.

"Tell me what's next, Slick," he murmured against her shoulder. "Tell me where this is going. It's your call."

Aimee flexed her fingers as the sensations whirled over her, memories with them. Of how wonderful it could be between them, how exciting. She hadn't been with a man since Hunter, hadn't had the desire. But now, desire curled through her, impossibly heavy, unbearably hot. She leaned voluntarily against the siding, giving him more room to touch her, telling him without words what she wanted.

Hunter unfastened the button that held up her halter top, then peeled the fabric slowly away. The cool night air kissed her breasts a moment before he did. As his mouth touched her flesh, she arched into him, a soft cry of pleasure shuddering past her lips.

"So beautiful," he murmured, cupping her breasts, lifting them for his mouth.

He caught one erect nipple, laving, nipping, then the other. She squeezed her eyes shut. It had been so long since a man had touched her. Since this man had touched her. She loved him, she always had. Hopeless or not, she was his.

Aimee arched more, higher, wanting to increase the contact of his mouth on her flesh. She stood on tiptoe, not realizing at first that he was pulling away from her.

Confused, she opened her eyes and found him gazing at her. Waiting. "What?" she whispered, curving her hands around his neck, clinging to him. "Why...did you...stop?"

Hunter searched her expression. He saw her longing, her confusion. He brought a hand to her cheek and stroked. She tipped her face into the caress and his chest tightened almost unbearably. She was so beautiful. So sweet and giving. If only he were a free man. Free from the past, from pain.

He could take what she offered, but not without first giving her a choice. An out. He would never be able to forgive himself if he did otherwise.

"I'm not going to make love to you just because you're willing," he murmured, his voice thick with desire. "It wouldn't be fair. To either of us." His slid his hands to her hair. The inky strands slid over and through his fingers. "Nothing is really changed, Aimee. And we're both going to have regrets. If we do make love...if we don't. It's a matter of degree."

He placed his hands over her breasts once more, acknowledging that depending on her answer, it may be for the last time. "I know what I want, Aimee. What about you? Do you know what you want?"

Aimee gazed back at him. She should say no. She should tell him goodbye. But she wanted this man. He was the only man she'd ever wanted. And tomorrow could be too late.

She covered his hands with her own. "Make love with me," she whispered. "I want us to be lovers again."

"Thank God," Hunter murmured, releasing a pent-up breath he hadn't even realized he held. "I was afraid you'd say no."

"How could I?" She smiled tremulously. "You were right. When you touch me I can deny you nothing."

With a sound of triumph, Hunter lowered his mouth to hers.

Their lips met and parted, their tongues twined and tasted. He wrapped his fingers in her hair, she threaded hers through his.

"It's been so long," he muttered against her lips, urgency clawing at him.

"So long," she repeated, just as impatient. "Love me, Hunter. Love me."

His hands were everywhere then, molding, frantic with wanting, frantic from the wait. He tugged up the full skirt of her dress and slid his hand underneath. Aimee moaned against his mouth as he roamed his hand up the back of her thigh, then around to the front. She moaned again as he found her.

Hunter drew in a deep breath, desperate for control. Her skin was incredibly warm, unbelievably smooth. And impossibly, she was ready for him.

Groaning, he took her mouth. He had no control. He'd waited too long—another minute would be an impossibility, another moment agony. Curling his fingers around the waistband of her panties, he yanked them over her hips and down.

Hunter retrieved the scrap of lace and slipped it into his pocket, then pressed her back against the wall. He found her once more, sinking his fingers into her moist center. She cried out and arched against his hand.

A frenzy of passion took them. Aimee fumbled with the snap of his jeans, with the zipper. He dragged her with him toward the porch swing. He bumped into the swing, his beer can went flying, striking the gallery floor and rolling, the sound high and sharp in the darkness.

Hunter sank onto the porch swing. "Come here, Slick."

He held out his hands. Without hesitation, she caught them, her breath coming in short, frantic pants. She laced her fingers with his and climbed onto him. The chains groaned, the chair creaked; she threw her head back as he thrust into her.

The first regret registered; Aimee forced it from her mind. For now, for tonight, she would forget about the past and the future. For this moment, they were without a history.

She grabbed the back of the chair and one of the chains, anchoring herself to him. Anchoring herself to the real world as passion spun her to the ozone and beyond. Hunter thrust again; the chair dipped crazily. He thrust again; she gripped the chain tighter and thrust back.

She caught his mouth, nipping at his lips, murmuring endearments she knew she shouldn't. Endearments he was not yet ready to hear.

The chair screamed a protest; Hunter caught her hips. With a cry of pleasure, Aimee collapsed against him. For long moments, the chair rocked, slowing as their hearts did. The squeak of the chains easing as their frantic breathing eased. Finally, save for the rustle of the breeze and the sounds of the night, all was still, quiet.

Aimee buried her face into the curve of Hunter's neck. What had she done? How could she have forgotten the lesson of the past? How could she have forgotten the pain?

He had offered her nothing. And wouldn't, she knew. He had nothing to give.

Hunter moved his hands over her back, up to her shoulders and neck, moving his fingers in gentle circles. "Regrets already?"

She squeezed her eyes shut, refusing to look at him. "No."

With gentle fingers, Hunter turned her face to his. He looked deeply into her eyes. "Liar."

A smile tugged at the corners of her mouth despite the ache inside her. "How come you've always been able to read my mind but I've never been able to read yours?"

He rubbed his nose against hers. "Not your mind, love. Your body." He moved his hands back to her shoulders and kneaded. "You went from liquid to cement in a matter of seconds." He laughed softly. "Stop that."

"Yes, Doctor." She rubbed her cheek against his hair, doing as he asked, allowing her worries to slip away from her. "Look," she whispered, reaching around him and plucking a cluster of star-shaped blossoms from the brush at the edge of the gallery.

"Jasmine." She held it to her nose, breathing deeply. "No wonder the scent's so potent here."

"No wonder," Hunter repeated.

She held it to her nose once more, growing dizzy on the flower's perfume, wishing she could somehow freeze this moment in time.

But the moment passed, and Hunter eased her off his lap and began to readjust his clothing. Aimee watched him, hurt. His instant retreat told her more than any words could, and she felt it like a slap. Turning away from him, she quickly covered herself, too.

"I should go in," she said, working to sound casual.

"Go in?" Hunter repeated, meeting her eyes, smiling wickedly at her. "I don't think so." He hauled her back onto him. "You're coming with me."

She looked at him in surprise. "I am?"

"You are."

She arched her eyebrows, hurt forgotten. "And if I refuse?"

"You won't."

"Overconfident, arrogant—"

"Hold on, Slick." Hunter stood and slipped his arms underneath her legs and lifted her. She wrapped her arms around his neck and nuzzled her face into his hair. Quietly, he carried her across the gallery and down the steps.

"Where are you taking me?" she asked.

"To my bed. Where you belong."

"Mmm." She smiled. "You sounded like a chauvinist barbarian just now. In fact, for the last few minutes."

"I'm doing my best."

She shook her head, her smile broadening. "I have legs, you know. And feet. Why don't you save your energy and let me walk?"

He laughed. "And blow my barbarian image. No way."

So Aimee let him carry her. And when they reached his room, his bed, she let him toss her on it and stand over her like a conquering hero.

"What now?" she whispered, already knowing.

"What do you think?"

His naughty grin sent delicious tremors up her spine. She held out her arms. "Come here, Hunter."

Chapter Nine

This time they savored. They kissed each other slowly... long drugging exchanges that left them both breathless. They touched and explored, they took the time to murmur approval, pleasure, need.

Hunter peeled away the halter dress, exploring each secret place he uncovered, delighting in her softness, her warmth. In the things that were all woman, but uniquely Aimee: the mole just south of her bikini line, the silky-soft ticklish spot behind her knee, the sound she made when he kissed that spot—and others.

Aimee, too, explored. She ran her hands over the planes of his body, the angles so different from her own curves. She reveled in those ways in which he was different, mysterious and male. And in the things that made him Hunter: the scent of his skin after lovemak-

ing, rich and musky; the feel of his crisp hair against
the sensitive flesh of her palm, the way his breathing
deepened to a rasp at the height of arousal.

She remembered it all. Everything. Every texture and
taste, the exact place and way to touch him and steal his
breath. And she delighted in doing just that, feeling a
sense of power in it. Feeling womanly and beautiful.
As she hadn't felt in a long time.

And never with any other man.

Hunter murmured her name as she used her mouth
and tongue to excite him. She smiled. In this way they
had no secrets, had nothing to hide from one another.
In the bedroom they had always been perfectly
matched.

Hunter brought her lips back up to his, then rolled
her onto her back. She wrapped her fingers in his hair
as he pleasured her with his mouth, loving her breasts,
the nip of her waist, her flat abdomen, moving even
lower. Aimee arched, the breath shuddering past her
lips, waves of pleasure crashing over her.

She tightened her fingers in his hair, clutching at
him. Their lovemaking was the same as before, she realized. Yet different. Different because there was a
desperation between them now. She felt it in the taut-
ness of his muscles, in the crackle of nervous energy
that hadn't existed back then. She felt it in her own
breathlessness. Her own fear.

He'd hurt her. Three and half years ago she wouldn't
have believed that possible. Now she knew better. Now
she knew just how badly he could hurt her.

But with the fear came longing. A longing enriched
by denial. An emotional resonance like never before.

With a sound of urgency, Hunter parted her thighs and entered her. Aimee wrapped her arms and legs around him, holding on to him more tightly than she ever had before. This act, she thought dazedly, meant something. Contained in it was the essence of life. Of immortality. It wasn't for strangers or mere acquaintances. It wasn't to be taken lightly.

She was a grown-up now, she realized. A woman making love with the only man who had ever made her happy. The only man she'd ever truly wanted.

And the one man who could shatter her into a million pieces.

Hunter whispered heated hungry words against her mouth, and the ability to think became an impossibility. All was sensation, perfect but fleeting. Both panted, catching one another's cries of pleasure, their bodies growing slick with sweat, unbearably hot with the act of love.

Hunter pressed her deeper into the mattress; she curled herself tighter around him. Taking her mouth, he claimed her. And she claimed him.

And then it was over. The breeze tumbled through the window, stinging their damp flesh. Aimee shivered, and Hunter released her long enough to pull the quilt from the foot of the bed and cover them.

"Warm enough?" he asked as she snuggled against him.

"Mmm-hmm." She smiled sleepily and pressed a kiss to his shoulder. "Perfect."

"I'm glad." He brushed at her damp hair. "Are you going to stay the night?"

The question struck her oddly. She tipped her head back and searched his gaze, telling herself she was being oversensitive, but bothered anyway. "Do you want me to?"

"How can you ask?"

How could she not? she wanted to shout. She was afraid. She hadn't a clue what the light of morning would bring for them.

But she kept those things to herself. "I *am* asking, Hunter. Do you want me to stay?"

"Yes," he murmured, drawing her mouth to his. "I do."

"Then I will," she whispered, sadness stealing over her. It was ending already, and it had just begun.

Aimee looked away, tears pricking the back of her eyes. She simultaneously cursed them and prayed they wouldn't spill over.

"Hey..." Hunter frowned and tipped her chin up, forcing her to meet his eyes once more. A soft smile tugged at his mouth. "So serious. What's going on in there?"

Aimee ignored his question, asking one of her own instead. "Did you ever think the crazy girl you knew in California would become such a serious-minded woman?"

He brought her hand to his mouth and kissed her fingers, one after the other. "I always took you seriously, Aimee."

"I know." And she did. Never once had she felt he didn't respect and admire her or her work. Something quite different had destroyed their relationship. "But... do you think I've changed?"

This time it was he who looked away in thought. When he met her eyes once more, his were soft with memories. "When I saw you again for the first time, I felt guilt and regret at the way you'd changed. I mourned for the reckless and carefree girl I'd known. I wondered where she'd gone. I wondered what part I'd played in her disappearance."

The tears pricked again, and she blinked furiously. Against them, against the hurt welling inside her. She inched her chin up a fraction, waiting for his next words.

"But now," he murmured, propping himself on an elbow and gazing down at her, "I no longer yearn for the 'old Aimee.' Now, I can't imagine you any way but the way you are. You've grown, you've matured. Some of the blush has been erased by experience. But it's been replaced by a richness, a depth that wasn't there before."

The tears in her eyes welled and brimmed over. He caught one with his index finger. It trembled there a moment before rolling off and being absorbed by the bedding. "Experience has changed you. That's part of living. To regret, to go back, is to deny life." He smiled sadly. "Time marches on."

Time marches on. Those words had tumbled around her head all night, interfering with her sleep, her dreams. And now, as the cool light of dawn stole across the bed, they were still on her mind.

Time. Aimee gazed at Hunter while he slept. What would today bring? she wondered. Love everlasting?

Despair? Regrets? And if they made it through this day, what of tomorrow and the day after that?

She loved him, more deeply than she ever had—because she understood now the transitory nature of happiness, of life. Oliver had begun to love him, too. They could be happy together. They could be a family.

If Hunter wanted them. Enough to let go of the family he had once had. And lost.

Aimee propped herself on an elbow and studied him, moving her gaze over his strong jaw, the subtle cleft in his chin, the tiny lines radiating from the corners of his eyes. He looked younger in sleep. Without the ghosts that often clouded his eyes and expression.

She reached out and touched his cheek, rough with his morning beard. What was it about this man, with his secrets and his pain, that called to her so deeply? Why, after all the time that had passed, and all the ways he had hurt her, hadn't she been able to let him go? He'd always been able to touch her in places and ways that no other man had been able to.

She wished it weren't so. She wished she could change. But wishing, like dreaming, was a childish waste of time and energy.

Aimee brushed her fingers through his hair, noticing for the first time a hint of gray in the golden strands. Hunter moaned and stirred, and she quickly withdrew her hand. She wasn't ready to face him. She wasn't yet prepared to do what she had to do.

Ask him his feelings. Tell him hers. Ask him if there was a chance for them.

Aimee squeezed her eyes shut. She needed a few more minutes to compose herself. To gather her thoughts. Her courage.

She wasn't yet ready for honesty. Not his. Not her own.

Outside the window a mourning dove cooed. Slipping out of bed, Aimee wrapped the old quilt around her and crossed to the window. The day beyond was bright and dewy, full of hope, of promise. If only she felt the same way.

"You look so sad."

Aimee turned. Hunter gazed at her, his blue eyes unclouded by sleep. How long had he been awake? she wondered. "Do I?"

"Yes."

"Maybe it's the new day," she murmured, turning back to the window.

Hunter sat up and shifted his own gaze to the window and the light beyond. "You never used to dislike the dawn."

"It's not the dawn. It's the tomorrow." She looked over her shoulder at him. "It's early. I didn't mean to wake you."

"You didn't. I always wake about this time. It's like I have an alarm clock inside." He made a sound that was at once bitter and resigned, and crumpled the sheet in his fist. "Perverse, because *I* do hate the dawn."

Surprised, Aimee turned fully back to him. He'd caught her off guard. This was something she hadn't known, hadn't suspected. "But, when we lived together... sometimes you would still be in bed when I awakened."

He smiled tightly. "I'd be back in bed after hours up prowling the quiet house." He shrugged. "It's been this way for years now. Since Ginny and Pete's...since the fire."

"I'm sorry."

He didn't respond and Aimee had the sense that he was suddenly far away from her, from this room. He stared at the window, toward the day beyond. The dove cooed again, the sound lonely against the light.

"Always another dawn," he said, almost to himself. "Another day without them. Having to face the light, having to admit they were gone. Having to face my failure, my guilt. My culpability in their deaths."

"Culpability?" Aimee drew her eyebrows together. "What do you mean?"

He returned his gaze to hers, his eyes dark with pain. With remembering. "It's my fault they died."

"But...the house caught on fire. The wiring...you sued the builder. You won." She shook her head. "Hunter—"

"The wiring was the reason the house caught fire." He curled his hands into fists. "They died because they couldn't get out of the house. The firemen found their bodies right inside the front door. The keys were in Ginny's hand."

"Oh, God." Aimee brought a hand to her mouth. "Hunter, how horrible. I'm so...sorry."

"I was an arrogant bastard. Nothing bad had ever happened to me. Growing up, my entire family was blessed. No money problems or illnesses. No deaths. Nothing. Somewhere along the line I started to believe that people caused their own tragedies. I would look at the bad things that happened to other people, other families, and think they had somehow earned their unhappiness.''

Hunter lowered his gaze. "I believed that if I did everything right, no tragedy could touch my family. I did everything right, and my family died."

Aimee crossed to the bed and knelt down beside it. She covered his hands with her own. "Accidents happen. Bad things come our way. It's part of life."

"Right." He met her eyes. His were dry but filled with a private anguish. A hell he had never shared with anyone before. "I went against the advice of my architect and had double dead-bolt locks installed. I wanted the extra protection. Problem is, in an emergency it takes time to find the key, to fit it into the lock. To get the hell out. That's a lot to ask when you're confused and terrified and breathing in smoke. When your little boy is screaming and . . ."

Emotion choked him, and Aimee climbed onto the bed and curved her arms around him. "It wasn't your fault, Hunter. It wasn't."

He didn't reply, and Aimee cupped his face in her palms. He looked at her, his expression tight with control. She pressed her mouth to his. "Ginny wouldn't have wanted you to spend your life second-guessing. She didn't blame you. I know she didn't. How could she? You only did what you thought best for your family."

"Yeah, I did that all right. The best."

Aimee buried her face in the crook of his neck, her arms still wrapped around him. For long moments, she just held him. Silently. No pressure, no demands.

After a time, he drew a shuddering breath. "I wanted you to know...everything. I wanted you to know why."

Her chest tightened. He wanted her to know why he didn't—and couldn't—love her. Why he couldn't love Oliver. Why he had shut himself off from the world of the living.

But he'd never confided in her before. Never opened up. That he had now, filled her with hope. That he had, meant something. Even if he didn't yet realize it.

She wouldn't force her feelings upon him; she wouldn't demand to know his. Not yet. She loved him. She could wait.

She tipped her head back to meet his eyes. "Nothing you said changes the way I feel about you."

"I wish it did." He rested his forehead against hers. "I'm no good for you, Aimee. You know that."

She took a deep breath. "Then leave, Hunter. Last time I made the break. This time it's up to you."

Hunter didn't leave. Although over the next week Aimee could tell he thought about it constantly. It was there in the faraway expression that would sometimes come into his eyes, in the way he looked at her or Oliver, when he thought she couldn't see—sadly, as if he'd already said good-bye.

Aimee plumped her bed pillows, then tossed them back into place. Despite that and a niggling sense of doom she chose to ignore, they'd had fun. They'd laughed and played, taking Oliver to the park and swimming and to the zoo in New Orleans.

They'd done many other things together as well, the three of them, like a family. Roubin had been more than happy to take total responsibility for the store, and Aimee knew her father thought her and Hunter's future together a given. She wished she could be so positive.

Aimee turned toward her bedroom window and the sweet morning breeze that tumbled through. The lace curtains stirred with it, and she reached out and touched one. May was drawing to a close already. It hardly seemed possible that summer was almost here.

Time marches on.

Hunter couldn't stay indefinitely.

Aimee pushed that thought from her head, thinking instead of the last week. She and Hunter had made love whenever and as often as they could slip away, and always after Oliver had gone to sleep for the night. They had reveled in each other, in rediscovering themselves and their relationship through the physical act of love.

And afterward they had talked. For hours and on subjects she hadn't discussed in years: national and international politics; art and issues, such as the environment and animal rights. She'd forgotten that part of having Hunter in her life. She'd forgotten how much they'd seen eye-to-eye and how much fun it had been arguing when they hadn't.

More than once their arguments had led to laughter, laughter to another round of lovemaking.

Aimee smiled to herself. It had been exhilarating. She felt more alive than she had since coming home.

Oliver, too, seemed to be blossoming. He had become more loquacious, more independent and courageous under Hunter's tutelage. Her baby had grown up, just a bit. She saw now that Hunter had been right. In small ways she'd been holding him back by being overprotective, too cautious.

She rubbed the antique lace between her fingers, her smile fading. It was almost frightening to realize how quickly Hunter had become a part of their lives, how quickly they had come to feel like a family.

What would it feel like when he was gone?

"Maman?"

Aimee turned and smiled at her son. He was still in his pj's, his hair still tousled with sleep. "Hi, baby. I bet you're ready for breakfast."

He shuffled into her bedroom, dragging his baby quilt behind him. "Mr. Hunter here?"

Aimee hesitated, a catch in her chest. She could see the concern—and hope—in her son's eyes. Lately, he would almost panic when he couldn't find Hunter. As if he, too, knew their time together was limited.

She'd told herself she would have to deal with her son's feelings for Hunter soon. She was afraid *soon* had come.

She took a step toward Oliver, smiling again. "Mr. Hunter's making some calls. Remember," she said gently, "he has a business in California. That's where he lives."

Oliver pouted, clearly not comprehending. "But he here."

"He's only visiting, honey." She struggled to keep her own tone calm, reassuring. "He'll have to go home soon."

"Oliver go, too?"

"No, baby." She shook her head. "I don't think so."

"Yes." Oliver drew his mouth up into a pucker. "Want to go with."

Aimee bent and held out her arms. "Come to Maman."

"No." His shook his head, his eyes bright with tears. "Want for my daddy."

Aimee pulled in a deep, steadying breath, her heart turning over. What could she say to him? It was what she wanted, too. And it hurt like hell. Because she couldn't give this to her son. And because, if she'd handled this situation differently, he wouldn't have had to go through this.

Damn Hunter anyway, she thought, suddenly angry. His inability—or unwillingness—to let go of the past was hurting them all. Oliver deserved better than that. So did she. If Hunter couldn't love them, he should just go.

As quickly as her temper had flared, it died. Aimee drew in another deep breath. But she didn't want to force him into a decision, because she couldn't bear to say goodbye. Not just yet.

"I ask him."

Aimee dragged her attention back to her son. "Oh, Oliver... baby, I don't think that's a good idea. Mr. Hunter's home is in California. He'll be leaving soon."

"No." Oliver's chin wobbled. "Don't want him to go."

Aimee crossed to her son and scooped him into her arms. He curved his own around her, his little body trembling with childish fury and disappointment.

She stroked his back and murmured comforting sounds. She had seen this coming; it had been inevitable from the moment she had looked out the screen door to see Oliver playing with Hunter. It didn't hurt any less for being so.

He whimpered, and she pressed a kiss to the top of his head. "I know, baby. I want him to stay, too. But that might not be possible. We'll just have to wait and see."

Hunter stood just outside the doorway and watched Aimee and Oliver, his chest heavy and aching. He felt cornered. Trapped. Not by Aimee, but by the situation. By his own indecision.

He wanted to stay. Lord, how he wanted to. But his want was selfish. He had nothing to give Aimee. Or Oliver. The longer he stayed, the more he hurt them.

Then why couldn't he bring himself to leave?

He would be forced into a decision soon. His partners in the clinic were getting desperate, even threatening to come down and physically bring him back. He could understand their frustrations—it wasn't fair to have dumped his entire work load on them just because he had to straighten out his life.

Was that what he was doing? Hunter wondered, looking back at Aimee and Oliver, guilt sawing through him. Was he working out his own problems, or just making more problems for them?

Listening to Oliver now, the answer seemed obvious. He stepped back from the doorway, not wanting Aimee or Oliver to see him just yet. Oliver wanted him to stay. He wanted him to be his daddy.

Daddy. Hunter flexed his fingers, the word running over him, filling his head. It made him feel strange. At once warm and jittery, pleased and terrified. Nobody but Pete had ever called him Daddy; he'd thought nobody ever would again. But here was Oliver and an opportunity he'd never expected to have again.

He drew his eyebrows together. Could he ever be the kind of father Oliver deserved? Could he ever love him? Hunter looked back at the mother and son. And what of Aimee? She deserved a man who could love her wholeheartedly and without ghosts. Could he ever be that man?

He doubted it. He doubted he had the capacity for any of it. That part of him had died with Ginny and Pete.

And yet... Hunter brought a hand to his hair and dragged it through. He'd changed since being here. He'd begun to feel again, begun to see life as more than just existing from one day to the next.

He didn't want to go, Hunter admitted. He didn't want to say goodbye. Not to Aimee. Not to Oliver. And not to the way he had begun to feel. Alive.

Aimee looked up then, and their eyes met. His chest tightened. He had to make a decision, he acknowledged. And soon. Aimee had been right—the longer he stayed, the more it would hurt Oliver when he left. The more it would hurt Aimee. And he'd already hurt Aimee enough to last a lifetime.

Yet, he couldn't bring himself to say the one word he needed to—*goodbye.*

Even as the word rang through his head, she smiled. The curving of her lips was soft and sweet, filling him like a song. He couldn't leave, not yet, not today. Pushing aside worries of the future, and fears of the past, Hunter moved toward her.

Chapter Ten

"Look, Russ," Hunter said into the receiver, "I'm sorry. But I still have some things to take care of here. You'll have to handle it."

Aimee stood behind the cash register, ostensibly checking out a customer, but in fact listening to Hunter. She handed the woman her change. "Thank you. Come again."

The woman looked at her strangely, then turned and walked away. After a moment, Aimee realized why—the woman was Mrs. St. Roche, whom she'd known all her life. And Aimee had acted as though she'd never seen her before. Aimee shook her head. The news that she'd lost her marbles would be all over town by sundown.

She would have to tell her father to expect a worried call from Tante Marie or one of the other relatives. Shutting the cash drawer, Aimee turned her attention back to Hunter and his call.

"No," Hunter continued, obviously frustrated, "I can't give you an exact date. I wish I could." He paused a moment, obviously listening, then exploded, "No, dammit! I can't tell you that, either. It's personal."

Aimee realized her hands were shaking and stuffed them into her pockets. She didn't know how much longer she could go on this way. Wondering if each day would be the one when Hunter decided to leave. Wondering how much time she had left with him. She felt as if she were living on a time clock, where each minute that ticked past might be her last with Hunter.

She'd established the rules of the game; she'd told him he would have to be the one to leave, he would have to make the break this time. Now her own rules were making her crazy.

She frowned. His feelings hadn't changed. He still held himself back from her emotionally. From Oliver. She felt his doubts, his reserve, as keenly as if he'd spoken them. They hurt. Almost as much as the hope clutching inside her.

"Maman?"

Aimee dragged her gaze from Hunter, and looked down at her son. She forced a smile. "Yes, baby?"

"Want to go fishing."

"Not now," she murmured, her attention slipping back to something Hunter was saying. "Maybe later."

"Want to go now." He stuck out his jaw stubbornly.

"No," she said sharply. "Maman said no."

His face puckered with hurt and regret curled through her. It wasn't fair to take out her frustration on Oliver. This situation wasn't one of his making, nor could he be immune to her tension. She ruffled his hair. "Maman will take you later. After lunch."

"No!" Oliver stomped his foot. "Want to go now."

Aimee stared at her son, shocked at his display of bad temper. Oliver had always been an easygoing child, his tantrums few and far between. And she certainly wasn't up for one right now.

"Oliver," she said sternly, "I said I would take you later. But if you don't straighten up immediately, we won't go at all. Got that?"

Oliver glared up at her, his eyes narrowed with determination, his lower lip out in a pout.

"Now," she finished, "go play with your toys." For a moment, Aimee thought he was going to argue with her some more. Then he turned and marched off.

She sighed, battling the urge to chase after him, take him in her arms and hug him silly. She wanted to give him everything he asked for. But she couldn't, not if she also meant to do her job as a mother. Aimee sighed again. Oliver was testing her, she understood that. It was part of growing up. But understanding didn't make it any less wrenching.

Hunter hung up the phone and she looked back at him in time to see an expression of resignation cross his face. Fear, icy cold, washed over her. He was leaving. He'd made his decision.

She drew in a deep, calming breath and faced him. "So when are you going?"

"Excuse me?"

"When are you going home, Hunter?"

He looked away. "I haven't made a decision yet."

"I don't believe you."

He met her eyes once more, his hot with anger. "I haven't made a decision," he repeated slowly, carefully.

"And I'll be the first to know when you do. Right?"

Hunter made a sound of frustration. "Let's not talk about this now. Okay?"

The beginnings of temper began to burn inside her. If she were Oliver's age she would stick out her lip and stomp her foot. But she wasn't. She inched up her chin instead. "When then?"

"I don't know, Aimee." He held up his hands. "Just...not...now."

She crossed to him, stopping when she stood directly in front of him. She tipped her face up to his, anger, full-blown now, pulsing through her. "You can do better than that, Hunter. How about tonight? Or tomorrow? Next week maybe? I'll mark it on my calendar."

He narrowed his eyes. "What's with the sarcasm, Slick? If you've got something on your mind, just say it."

She began to shake. Wheeling away from him, she squeezed her eyes shut and breathed deeply through her nose. When she turned back to him, she had garnered a modicum of control. "Why are you still here, Hunter? What things do you still have to take care of?"

Hunter drew his eyebrows together in surprise. "What are you talking about?"

"You told Russ you still had some things to take care of here. What things? A settlement for Oliver? If that's it, I accept." She pushed her bangs away from her face. "Whatever you want to give him, whatever will ease your conscience is fine with me."

She started to walk away, he caught her elbow and swung her back around to face him. He searched her gaze. "Why are you acting this way? This morning everything was fine."

"Was it?" she muttered. "Was it really?"

He frowned. "I thought so."

"But you're not the one being left hanging, are you, Hunter? You're not the one who's going to be left with the messy cleanup. You're not the one waiting to hear about her future."

Hunter swore. "What do you want me to say to you?"

"How about the truth?" She took a deep breath. "It's not a question of *if* you're going to go, is it? It's a question of when you're going."

He met her eyes. In his she saw regret. And bittersweet longings. "You know I have to go back. I have the clinic. I can't just up and—"

"Let me rephrase, then." Angry, hurt, she balled her hands into fists. "It's not a question of if our affair is going to end. It's only a matter of when. Isn't that right, Hunter?"

"That's not—"

"I love you."

Hunter took a step back, his expression tight with denial.

Aimee sucked in a sharp breath. He didn't want her to love him. It was so much easier, so much neater, for him to pretend everything between them was light and breezy. Even though he knew better.

She wished she could play the outraged innocent. The hapless victim. She couldn't. She was as much a part of the charade as he.

"Why didn't you tell me?" he managed, his voice thick.

"I had my reasons. Among others, because I didn't want to pressure you."

He clenched his hands into fists. "I didn't want this to happen, didn't plan for it."

"But it doesn't change the fact that it has." She inched her chin up. "What are you going to do about it?"

"Aimee, *chère*..." Roubin wheeled in the store, looking around in confusion. "...what are you doing here?"

Aimee turned to her father, confused herself. "What do you mean, Papa? Am I supposed to be somewhere else?"

Roubin's face slackened, and he shifted his gaze from her to Hunter, then back. "My *petit-fils*...Oliver, he told me you were taking him fishing."

Aimee stared at her father, a tingling sensation starting at her forehead and moving down, numbing her. She shook her head to clear it, to throw off the sensation. "I told him I would take him after lunch."

"But...Oliver, he had his fishing pole."

She shook her head again, her heart thundering in her chest. "He knows not to go down to the water...without one of..." Her words trailed off. She thought of Oliver's expression when she'd told him no. Thought of his independence of late and of the way he'd stuck his chin out stubbornly.

"Oh, my God." She started for the door, Hunter with her. At a dead run, they slammed through the screen door and down the stairs, heading for the bayou.

Aimee was aware of her father following behind them, but she didn't pause or look back. "Oliver!" she called. "Where are you? Oliver! Answer your *maman!*"

Nothing.

"Where?" Hunter shouted.

"I don't...know. I—"

"Then guess, dammit!"

"Beside the house." She brought a hand to her throat, a dozen different prayers screaming through her head. "By the...the big cypress tree. We've fished there before."

Hunter shot past her. Aimee watched him, the sense of doom she'd been feeling for days weighing down on her. No, she told herself. Oliver wouldn't go to the water alone. He knew the danger. She'd been drumming that into his head since he'd been old enough to listen.

Aimee sucked in a deep breath, trying to hold hysteria at bay. They were afraid for nothing. They would find him safe in his room, playing with his toys. Safe. He would be...

* * *

Oliver floated facedown in the bayou.

A cry ripped from Aimee's throat, high and tight, rending the peaceful morning air. "No!" she screamed. "Oliver!"

Hunter hit the water at a run and it splashed up around him, the drops glistening in the sun like tears. Sobbing, Aimee reached the water's edge as Hunter scooped up Oliver and carried him head down from the water.

To drain the water from his lungs.

Aimee brought a hand to her mouth to hold back a cry. *He wasn't breathing. Her baby wasn't breathing.*

"Call 911," Hunter shouted to Roubin, who was already wheeling up the gallery ramp. "Call 911, then bring a pillow and a blanket!"

Aimee heard her father's answering shout as if from a great distance. She dropped to her knees beside Oliver. How many minutes had it been? she wondered, the hysteria rising inside her. How long was too long? A sob caught in her throat. She couldn't lose him. She couldn't.

She wrapped her arms around herself, rocking back and forth as she watched Hunter press his mouth over Oliver's face, breathing for him, waiting a moment then repeating the procedure again. And again.

"*Chère* . . . Oliver, he is all right?"

Aimee looked up, tears streaming down her face. Her father wheeled toward them, a pillow and blanket on his lap. She opened her mouth, but couldn't voice her fears.

He stopped beside her, and she reached her hand up. He clasped it, his big, callused hand closing around hers like a hug. "Hold on, Aimee. The ambulance, she is coming."

Aimee nodded and turned back to Oliver. What would she do if she'd lost him? How would she go on?

Oliver coughed. Aimee cried out in relief and caught his hand. He was alive. Her baby was alive.

"Thank God," Roubin murmured, crossing himself. In the distance the ambulance wailed. Oliver's lids fluttered open; he coughed again.

Aimee brought his hand to her cheek, to her mouth. His skin was alarmingly cold and clammy. She rubbed his hand between hers. "Maman's here, Oliver. You're going to be fine. Hold on... baby. Hold on."

"Don't expect too much right now," Hunter said, the sound tight with strain. "He's in shock." Hunter looked up at Roubin; the older man tossed him the pillow, then the blanket.

Hunter placed the pillow under Oliver's feet, then laid the blanket over him, tucking it carefully around him. The ambulance sounded closer. Hunter smiled tenderly and stroked Oliver's head. "You're going to be all right, Tiger. You're going to be all right."

The next minutes were a blur. The ambulance arrived and the paramedics raced down to the bayou with a stretcher. While they loaded Oliver onto the stretcher and carried him to the waiting ambulance, Hunter conferred with them.

Aimee and Hunter didn't speak to each other during the race to the hospital. They sat on either side of Oliver, each clasping one of the boy's hands, each murmuring comforting words. Once they'd looked up simultaneously and their eyes had met. They'd just stared at one another, a curious emptiness between them. As if, in the aftermath of what they'd just been through, they had nothing left to give one another.

It shouldn't be that way, she thought several hours later, gazing at her sleeping son. They should have clung to one another, should have provided each other solace from the pain.

Tears welled in her eyes. She'd almost lost Oliver. She'd almost lost her baby. She ran her gaze over him. He looked terrifyingly pale, even against the white hospital sheets. But not blue, she thought, shuddering at the memory.

The image of Oliver floating facedown in the water filled her head, and she hugged herself. That image would haunt her dreams forever, she knew. She doubted she would be able to sleep tonight, or sleep well for a long time.

Bending over the bed, she pressed a kiss to Oliver's forehead, saying a silent prayer of thanks to *le bon Dieu* for letting her keep her baby. It wasn't the first prayer she'd said since Oliver had come back to life, coughing up the bayou, and it wouldn't be her last. No amount of thanks would ever be enough.

From behind her, Aimee heard Oliver's door open. She turned; her eyes met Hunter's. He stood in the doorway, his eyes dark with grief, his expression tight with strain.

He'd been terrified. She'd seen it, felt it. The fear had emanated from him in waves, even though he'd kept his composure, doing what he'd had to do in order to save Oliver.

She owed him her thanks. Without his quick, cool thinking, she might have lost her son. She liked to think that if Hunter hadn't been there she would have kept her wits, done whatever necessary to save her child. But she couldn't know for sure.

She intended never to find out.

"How is he?" Hunter asked.

"Sleeping." She squeezed her eyes shut, against fatigue and a lingering fear. And against the image of Oliver in the water. "The doctor wants to keep him overnight. To watch him."

Hunter nodded. "I think that's best."

She clasped her hands together. "I'm staying with him. They're going to move a cot into his room. I wouldn't want him to awake in the night . . . and worry that—"

"Sure." Hunter shifted his gaze from hers to Oliver. "Roubin's on the phone, calling to see how Oliver's faring. Want me to tell him you'll call later?"

"No. I'll take it." She looked back down at Oliver, then back at Hunter. "If he wakes up—"

"I'll tell him you'll be right back."

"Thanks."

She started to move by him; Hunter caught her arm. "Aimee?"

She met his eyes, hers full of questions. For long moments he gazed at her, all the things he wanted to say swelling to near bursting inside him. He dropped her hand. "I'm glad he's safe, Aimee," he whispered. "So glad."

She nodded, tears filling her eyes. Without another word, she went to get the phone.

Hunter watched her as she left the room, helplessness pulling at him. Resignation. A man didn't admit fear. A man had to be strong, invincible. Ready to take on the world. He hadn't felt invincible in a long time. He hadn't felt whole.

He drew in a steadying breath. Aimee deserved a whole man. So did Oliver.

He wished for a different ending anyway.

Hunter turned toward the bed. Oliver slept, his breathing light but regular, a hint of color—of life— tinting his cheeks. He'd never meant to stay so long. He hadn't meant to get attached. To Oliver. Or Roubin. To this place.

He'd already been attached to Aimee. He just hadn't realized it.

Hunter crossed to the bed and gazed down at the boy—his son. As he did, his heart swelled in his chest, pressing against his ribs and lungs, making it difficult to breathe. Oliver was a beautiful boy, special and bright. A miracle.

With a shaking hand, Hunter reached out and gently stroked Oliver's cheek. His skin was warm. Not cold and clammy as it had been when he'd pulled him out of the bayou.

"Thank God you're alive," Hunter whispered, brushing the boy's dark hair away from his forehead. "When I saw you there, in the water . . ."

Tears filled Hunter's eyes and choked his windpipe. He lifted his eyes heavenward, battling for control, finding it but at great cost. "It was so close," he continued. "Another minute, hell, another second, and we might have lost you."

Hunter cleared his throat, and looked back down at Oliver's sleeping face. "If you'd died, I don't think I could have made it. I think I would have just...died right there with you. I already lost one boy...I couldn't bear to lose another."

He smoothed the sheet and blanket, using the opportunity to touch Oliver for the last time, stalling to prolong the moment.

"I've got to go," he said finally. "I wanted you to know that I do...love you. I never thought I'd say that again, never thought I could feel that for another child.

"I want to stay, Oliver. I do. But I can't. You see..." With the heels of his hands, Hunter brushed at his cheeks, at the moisture he hadn't even known was there. "...I've got these ghosts. And they follow me around. I can't seem to shake them. And I can't be...whole because of them. I can't be fearless." He sucked in a deep breath. "You and your mom deserve somebody who can be both."

Hunter bent and pressed a kiss on Oliver's cheek. "I'm going to miss you...buddy. Be good. Take care of your mom. She's a really great lady. I..."

He bit back the words, unable to say them. Afraid that in voicing them, he would feel too much, open himself to too much. And, maybe, lose the courage to do what he had to. He squeezed his eyes shut, fighting for control.

"What's matter?" Oliver whispered. "Owie?"

Hunter opened his eyes to find the boy looking sleepily at him. Hunter stiffened, working to compose himself. He forced an easy smile. "Hey, Tiger. What are you doing awake?"

"Don't know." He yawned. "Where Maman?"

"On the phone with your *pépère*. She'll be right back."

"Why look so sad?"

"I'm not sad." He smiled again. "You're going to be all right. That's happy news."

Oliver lifted his hand to Hunter's, resting on the bed rail. He curled his little fingers around Hunter's larger ones. Hunter's breath caught and he returned the gesture, clinging to Oliver's hand. "You really gave us a scare," Hunter murmured, bending low over the bed. "Don't you do it again. Okay?"

"Not s'pposed to go down to bayou alone." Oliver yawned again, fighting sleep. "Maman's mad."

"No," Hunter whispered, stroking his hair. "She was really frightened, though. So was I. But she's not mad."

Oliver's eyelids drooped. "I . . . gla—"

"Me, too."

"Love . . . you . . ."

Oliver's fingers relaxed and slipped from Hunter's. For one long moment after the child was again asleep, Hunter continued to hold his hand. Then he gently released it and tucked the blanket around him.

Bending, Hunter pressed a kiss to his forehead. "Goodbye, Tiger. I . . . remember what I said. Okay?"

Aimee hung up the phone and went back to Oliver's room. She found Hunter beside Oliver's bed, gazing down at their son. Her heart turned over. *Their son.*

How wonderful that sounded to her, how warm; yet what a mockery it was.

She drew in a deep, shuddering breath, and pressed the heels of her hands to her eyes. Exhaustion pulled at her, as did leftover fear and a sort of hopelessness. She dropped her hands to her sides. "We need to talk, Hunter."

"Yeah, we do."

"Outside?"

He nodded and followed her out to the hallway. There, she drew another deep breath and faced him. "I can't go on this way."

As the words passed her lips, Aimee acknowledged surprise. She hadn't meant to say those words, in that way. They'd just popped out. And now that they had, she couldn't go back. She didn't want to.

"I love you, Hunter. But I can't go on the way we have been. Not knowing. Living on hope."

He tensed. At his sides, he fisted his fingers, as if waiting for a blow.

She crossed to him, stopping so close she smelled the sweat of fear on him, the scent of the bayou. She would never forget this moment, would always associate those smells with a biting sadness.

Tipping back her head, she met his eyes. "You were right. I've been hiding from life. Licking my wounds and feeling sorry for myself. Avoiding life because I hurt. Avoiding living so I wouldn't be hurt again."

She shook her head. "I can't go on that way. Not any more. It took almost . . . losing Oliver to make me see how precious life is. Every moment. I've been throwing it away. For nearly four years now."

Aimee reached up and touched Hunter's cheek lightly, then dropped her hand. She wanted to hold him, wanted his arms around her. They'd almost lost their son. They should be holding one another right now. Clinging to one another.

Instead, they were saying goodbye.

She searched his gaze. What would he do if she *did* turn to him now? she wondered. Would he be able to give her the support she needed? And if Oliver had...died, would Hunter have been there for her? She thought of their history, thought of the way they'd gazed at one another in the ambulance, and she shook her head.

It wasn't in him. Maybe once, a long time ago, but not any more.

Sadness moved over her. If she were to have a man in her life, she needed one she could lean on. And she needed one who would lean on her.

"Aimee, I—"

"No." She reached up and laid her index finger gently against his lips. "No apologies or excuses. No dialogue. Just tell me what you feel for me."

For long moments he gazed at her. "I don't want to say, Aimee. I don't want to hurt you."

And he would hurt her, Aimee realized, the last glimmer of hope dying inside her. Then there would be nothing left for them to say. And no reason for him to stay. The coward's way—for both of them—would be to just ... let it go. But she'd done that before, and it hadn't been final enough. She'd continued to hope.

Aimee inched her chin up. "I need to know, to hear, what you feel for me."

He caught her hands and brought them to his chest. Beneath them, she felt the thunder of his heart. When he spoke, his voice was filled with regret. "I think you're the most special woman in the world. I can't imagine turning and walking away from you, although I know..." He let the thought trail off and pressed her hand closer against his heart. "You make me...happy, Slick. You make me forget."

"But that's not love," she whispered, her voice thick with tears. "That's not enough." She swallowed against the emotion choking her. It took every ounce of her courage, her strength, to voice what she knew she must. "I know you don't love me now, but do you think...someday you...might?"

She saw the answer in his eyes. But it wasn't enough to see, to know, he had to tell her it was hopeless. If he didn't smash her hopes now, she might not be able to let him go. And to go on, to build a new life for herself and Oliver, she had to let him go.

"Today I almost lost Oliver. You almost lost Oliver. Our son. How did that make you feel?"

"How do you think?" Hunter exploded, then lowered his voice. "When I saw Oliver...in the water...I felt like my heart was being ripped from my body. Is that clear enough?"

"No." She eased her hands from his and crossed back to Oliver's hospital room. She peeked through the window at her sleeping son, then looked back over her shoulder at Hunter. "Do you love Oliver? The way a father loves a son? As much as you loved Pete?"

"My God, Aimee..." He dragged a hand through his hair, his expression stricken, trapped. "Why are you doing this?"

Aimee stared at Hunter. He didn't, she thought, her heart turning over. He never would. She brought a hand to her mouth, hurt moving over her in ever increasing waves.

He was going to leave her. Leave Oliver. It was over.

She made a sound of pain, and turned back toward the tiny window and her son beyond. How could he not love Oliver with his whole heart? After everything, how could he not love her? He didn't have a heart, she thought, anger pushing at her hurt. He preferred loneliness to living, preferred alienation to love.

This time, she wasn't going to just let go, Aimee thought angrily. This time she would say what she felt.

She swung back around, meeting his gaze furiously. "In the last weeks, you pushed me, Hunter. You badgered and bullied me. Into facing my feelings. My fears. Into facing life." She shook her head. "You pushed me to rediscover the woman I used to be, you pushed me to dream again."

She crossed the hall to stand before him once more. "What about you? You've been running, hiding, a lot longer than I have. From everything. Now you're getting ready to run from my love. From Oliver's. And from the way you feel about us."

She shook her head. "We could be a family. We could be happy. But you're too wedded to your own pain, your own misery, to have anything to give someone else. Why are you doing this, Hunter?"

"I'm sorry, Aimee." He took a step toward her, reaching out a hand, touching her cheek. "That I can't love you. That I can't give you what you need."

Aimee jerked away from his caress. "It's not that you can't. You won't."

Her eyes welled with tears, and she fought them back. "After today I can understand some of your pain. When I thought I'd...lost Oliver, the pain I felt...I can't even describe it. It felt like I had died, too.

"But understanding your pain doesn't change the fact that I want, that I deserve, more than a dead man. Deserve better than a man who's given up on life to avoid pain. All along you've been saying that to me. And you were right. But all along I thought I could bring you back to life. Just as I believed four years ago. If you'd let me. But you wouldn't let me then, and you won't let me now. And I'm not going to try any more.

"I want you to leave, Hunter. I've said that before but hoped you would stay. Not this time. I'm done living on hope. Unless you're willing to live and love, I want you to go."

For long moments they gazed at one another, then without speaking he turned and walked away.

Chapter Eleven

Hunter set his garment bag beside his car, then crossed to the gallery, where Roubin sat, a box of tangled lures in his lap.

He squinted up at Aimee's father, moving his gaze over his face. Today Roubin had almost lost his grandson. The experience had aged him. Hunter understood only too well how it could; he would never be the same either. "A bit hot to be sitting outside this afternoon."

"Me, I am used to the heat." The older man motioned to the garment bag. "You are going some place?"

Hunter climbed the steps, the carefully packed music box in his hands. "The time has come for me to go home."

"Pardon?" Roubin drew his eyebrows together as if he had heard incorrectly.

"My patients need me," Hunter replied, shifting his gaze to a point just left of the other man's shoulder. "My partners need me. I've been gone too long already."

"I see," Roubin said, clearly not seeing at all.

"Oliver's going to be fine," Hunter rushed on, uncertain whether needing to reassure himself or the other man. "There's been no apparent damage. He might have a fear of the water, but some children escape without even that."

"And what of you, *mon ami?"* Roubin asked softly. "How are you going to be?"

Hunter looked back at Roubin, surprised. "Me? I'm fine."

"Then why do you leave this way?"

"I told you, the time has come to go back. I've been away too long."

"Non." Roubin shook his head. "You can not go. Not like this. Aimee, she needs you. Oliver, your son, he needs you."

Hunter looked away, his chest unbearably tight. He fought for an even breath. "You don't understand, Roubin."

The older man snorted. "Aimee, too, she tells me I don't understand. All the time, she tells me this. What good is living to be an old man if no knowledge, no sight, comes with the age. *Le bon Dieu,* I do not think he has us grow old only to wither and die."

Hunter worked at a smile. He wondered if the curving of his lips looked as stiff as it felt. "I told you, I'm not a religious man."

Roubin inclined his head. "Yes, but those are words only. They are not what you believe. They are not what you feel, in your heart."

Emotion tightened in Hunter's throat once more. "I'm no good for her, Roubin."

"You and Aimee, you love each other. When there is love, how could it not be good?"

Hunter shook his head. "You're wrong. Sometimes it's bad. I have nothing to give her, Roubin. I never had." He tipped his face up to the cloudless sky, to the heavens beyond. "I wish I did."

Roubin snorted once more. "You are afraid. Because of what happened to your wife and son. You are afraid to feel too much. I can understand this, yes. But it is time to let go of the past, just as you advised me to do."

The image of Pete flew into his head, then the image of Oliver, floating facedown in the water. Oliver, his face blue from lack of oxygen, his heart and lungs still. Hunter sucked in a sharp breath, feeling as if he, too, was suffocating. As if he, too, had stopped breathing.

He had to go. He couldn't stay.

Hunter stiffened his spine and took a step away from the older man. "I'm sorry. I never meant to hurt her. Or Oliver."

"Then why are you?" Roubin demanded.

Hunter swore, refusing to think of Aimee's hurt. Of Oliver's. They would get over him, he told himself. They would go on to have a nice life, one free of his ghosts. A life with someone who could freely love them.

He would bring them nothing but unhappiness.

"If you need anything, if Aimee or Oliver needs anything, don't hesitate to call." Hunter held out one of his business cards. "Here are my numbers. If they need . . . anything, call me. Aimee won't want to, you know that. I'm depending on you to do this, Roubin."

Roubin gazed at his outstretched hand a moment, then nodded and took the card. *"Oui.* I will do this."

"I'm going to set up a college fund for Oliver. Aimee will agree. And even if she doesn't, it will be there." Hunter took another step back. "Well, I guess this is goodbye."

"So you will run away like the swamp dog?" Roubin frowned up at him. "I was wrong about you, *mon ami.* I thought you were a man."

Hunter stiffened, against the other man's words, against the way they made him feel. He hadn't realized just how much Roubin's respect had meant until this moment, until he'd lost it.

Hunter made a sound of frustration. He didn't have to justify himself to Roubin. He owed him no explanations.

Then why did he feel the urge to explain? To convince? And why did it bother him so much that he couldn't?

"I want Aimee and Oliver to have this," he said stiffly. He handed Roubin the packed music box. "She can do what she wants with it. Maybe Oliver . . ." Hunter's voice thickened, and he cleared his throat. "Goodbye, Roubin."

The older man didn't respond, and Hunter didn't hang around waiting for him to. Feeling as if he were leaving a piece of himself behind, maybe the most important piece, Hunter walked down the gallery steps for the last time.

When Aimee returned home the following day, Hunter was gone. She would have known, even if her father hadn't called her at the hospital with the news, even if she hadn't been the one who'd pushed Hunter into leaving. Everything felt different—quieter, emptier. Somehow gray.

She felt as if a part of her was missing.

She shook her head against the thought and moved her gaze around the store. It was unbelievable to her how accustomed she'd become to Hunter's presence, how much she'd grown to depend on seeing him. He'd fit so quickly into their lives, so easily.

He'd taken up residence in her heart with even less effort.

Aimee found her father's gaze, then looked away from the compassion in his eyes. She'd never announced her feeling, her love, for Hunter. Obviously, he'd known anyway.

Oliver squirmed out of her arms and raced for his grandfather. *"Pépère!"*

Roubin caught the boy to his chest, holding him tightly. "No worse for wear, eh?" he said, his voice thick with emotion.

"Hospital smelled funny." Oliver wrinkled his nose. "Yucky."

Aimee smiled. The invincibility of youth. After everything he'd been through, the two things that had made the biggest impression on her son had been the smell of the hospital and the green Jell-O they'd served with lunch.

"If you don't mind, Papa, I'd like to take Oliver over to the house for a while. Let him play with his toys and . . ."

Her voice trailed off, her smile faded. She met her father's eyes. On the counter by the cash register sat Hunter's music box.

"He left it for you. And Oliver."

Her legs trembling, Aimee crossed to it and touched the glass dome lightly. Her head filled with the memory of lying in bed with Hunter, of gazing into one another's eyes, the music box's melody filling the quiet. She blinked against the tears that stung her eyes. She would never be able to look at the beautiful box and not remember making love with Hunter.

Aimee drew her hand back from the glass and wrapped her arms around her middle. Why had he left it? She didn't want to remember, didn't want to spend another moment wishing for what would never be.

And yet, when she looked at the music box, she could do nothing but.

"I tried to get him to stay, *chère.*"

Aimee smiled sadly. "I know, Papa. It's okay. I'm going to be fine."

Oliver squealed, suddenly seeing the music box. "Wind, Maman." She did, and he slid off his grandfather's lap and raced over to it. For several moments he watched the belle circle the base, then looked back up at Aimee. "Where Mr. Hunter?" He looked around, his expression expectant.

Aimee took a deep breath and counted to ten. The moment she had been dreading had arrived. He would be hurt by Hunter's departure, and there was nothing she could do but tell him the truth. "Honey," she began gently, "Mr. Hunter had to go home."

Not listening, Oliver ran to the rear of the store, to the back door and yard beyond. A second later he trotted back, frowning. "Where Mr. Hunter?"

Aimee exchanged a worried glance with her father. "Come here, Oliver." She bent down and held out her arms. "Maman needs to talk to you."

Oliver started toward her, dragging his feet as if he knew what was coming and wanted to put off the inevitable. When he reached her, she scooped him into her arms and carried him out to one of the rocking chairs on the front gallery.

For several moments she rocked him silently, preparing her thoughts, using the moments and the gentle motion of the chair to lull him. "Mr. Hunter," she began softly, "went back to California. Remember, we talked about this. I explained about his business."

"No...no." Oliver shook his head. "Music box here."

"He left it for us. It's a gift." She forced a smile. "He knew how much you liked it."

Oliver's eyes filled and he shook his head again, this time vehemently, as if by denying reality, he could change it.

"Yes, baby. He's gone. He had to go."

"But...he no said goodbye to me."

"He did. At the hospital." She rubbed his back in soothing circles, wondering if Hunter really had. "You were sleeping."

Oliver drew in a trembling breath and hung his head. "I sorry," he whispered.

She nuzzled the top of his head. "For what, baby?"

"Going to water alone. Mr. Hunter left 'cause I bad boy."

"No." Aimee hugged her son tightly, hating that he blamed himself, hating herself for making his misery possible. "You're not a bad boy. And you had nothing to do with Mr. Hunter leaving. California is his home. It was time for him to go... home."

She squeezed Oliver tighter, the image of her son, face down in the bayou, filling her head. With the image came a choking fear. She battled it. Her son needed her now, he needed her strong and calm.

"Hunter was worried about you," she said softly. "So was your *pépère*. We were all very frightened. Promise me you'll never go down by the water without an adult again." She tipped his face up to hers and looked him in the eye. "Can you promise me that?"

He nodded, tears trembling on his lashes. "Promise, Maman."

She smiled with more confidence than she felt. "Good boy."

He looked up at her, his dark eyes hopeful. "Mr. Hunter come back now?"

"No, baby. He's not coming back."

"But... I no want him to go." He started to cry and pressed his face to her chest. "Want him to stay."

"I know." Aimee rubbed his back, letting him cry, struggling against the need to cry herself. She had wished for Hunter to stay, too. "But sometimes," she murmured as much to her son as to herself, "even when we want something more than anything, we can't have it."

"Why?" Oliver whispered, the sound muffled against her T-shirt.

Good question, she thought. If only she had a good answer. She kissed the top of his head. "It's just part of life, baby. Part of living."

"Oliver, he is going to be all right?" Roubin asked two nights later.

Aimee tucked the blanket around her son, then turned and faced her father, sitting in the doorway behind her. She knew her father referred not to Oliver's near drowning, but to his grief over Hunter's departure. Tears filled her eyes. The last couple of days had been difficult, in different ways, for them all. Even her father had seemed to be grieving.

She didn't fight or try to hide the tears in her eyes and voice. "He's hurt. He'd grown to love Hunter."

"We all did, *non?*"

"Yes." She drew a deep breath and expelled it slowly. "He thinks he's coming back. Because of the music box."

"I am sorry, *chère.* So sorry."

"Me, too."

"Come." Roubin motioned behind him. "Oliver, he will be fine. Let us talk."

Aimee nodded and stood. "I think that's a good idea, Papa. There are some things I need to discuss with you."

They went to the kitchen, moving side-by-side, Roubin wheeling himself. Only a few short weeks ago, she would have pushed him, and neither one of them would have questioned it. Now her father rarely asked for her help.

When they reached the kitchen, Aimee saw that he had made coffee and put out some of the cookies Tante Marie had brought by.

She looked at him in surprise, and he laughed. "This old man, he is still some good to you, *non?* He can still surprise his *petite-fille.*" He motioned to the table. "Sit . . . sit."

Aimee did, and Roubin poured her a cup of coffee and brought it to her. Her throat constricted at the pride and pleasure in his eyes as he handed her the cup.

She wrapped her hands around the steaming mug, finding the heat comforting despite the warm night. Hunter was responsible for her father's progress. In the weeks he had been with them, he had done so much for them. He'd changed their lives.

Would she ever be able to look at her father, accept a cup of coffee from him, and not remember? Not think of Hunter?

Bittersweet pain curled through her, and she sipped the coffee. She looked up to find her father watching her carefully, his expression worried. She smiled. "I'm fine, Papa. I am."

Flustered, he set his own mug on the table. "I am your father. I am entitled to worry."

Aimee laughed and gazed at her father with affection. It felt good sitting here with him like this, talking. When was the last time they'd shared a cup of coffee and a laugh? Too long.

She reached out and covered his hand with her own. "Oh, Papa, you never change."

"And this is bad?"

"Non," she said, falling into his patois. "It is good. *Très bon.*"

He curled his fingers around hers. "I love you, *chère*. I always have."

She returned the pressure of his fingers. "And I you, Papa."

"Bon." He eased his hand from hers and inched the cookie plate her way. "Eat. Marie, she says you are too thin."

"She does, does she?" Aimee murmured, grinning, but selected a cookie obediently. It did as much good to argue with Marie as it did with her father.

But, the time had arrived to become fully an adult. To live for herself, to make the choices she needed to— for herself and her own well being. And she needed to make a change. She needed to move forward with her life. It would affect her father. He would be hurt.

How could she make him understand that her need for change had nothing to do with him? Aimee broke off a piece of the cookie and tasted it, finding it rich and almost cloyingly sweet. She hated to hurt him; she'd disappointed him so often.

She caught her bottom lip between her teeth. She'd disappointed herself more.

"We are at a crossroads. I know this, *chère*. You do not need to worry over your old papa. He will understand."

Aimee looked up, surprised. She lifted her eyebrows in question.

He shook his head and chuckled. "I could always read you. Sometimes, I pretend otherwise because I do not like what I see. Just as sometimes you do not like to face the truth."

"We're so much alike."

Roubin nodded. *"Oui.* It has always been so."

Through the open window came the cry of an egret, the croak of a bullfrog. Aimee pushed her chair from the table, stood and crossed to look out. In the dark, she saw the flash of the fireflies. She thought of the summer nights of her childhood, of the hours spent chasing them. The days and nights had seemed endless then, yet now they slipped by so quickly, faster even than the wink of a firefly's light.

She reached out and touched the screen. "I had a wonderful childhood, Papa. I think of that girl sometimes, of her growing up here on the bayou, as much a part of this place as the jasmine or the egret. And yet, I always wanted something different. Always dreamed of some place else. I don't know why. I love it here. I love being near you and the rest of the family."

Aimee drew her hand back from the screen. "But I'm the same girl I was then, the same young woman who defiantly left La Fin," she continued quietly. "I have the same dreams. The same longings."

She looked over her shoulder at her father, smiling sadly. "For a while I gave them up. I told myself I'd been foolish to wish for something other than what I had, I told myself my dreams were foolish."

She turned back to the fireflies and their elusive light. "I told myself I believed what you'd told me so many times, that I belonged here and no place else. That I was wrong to leave."

"*Chère,* I—"

She turned her back to the night and faced her father fully. "Let me finish, Papa. This isn't easy for me. It'll be better if I just say it."

He inclined his head and folded his trembling hands in his lap.

"For a long time now," she continued, "I've been floundering. Not happy, but not unhappy, either. Hunter helped me...see that." Her throat closed, and she cleared it. "California was a disaster. Because of my love affair with Hunter and because my photography exhibit bombed. I ran home to lick my wounds. I ran home because I was afraid. For the first time in my life I'd failed. For the first time in my life I had no self-confidence."

Her father's lips lifted a little at that, and hers did, too. Growing up she had been self-confident to a fault. Her mother had always teased that in that way she was her father's daughter. In truth, she was his image in many ways.

"So here I was in La Fin. Licking my wounds. Hiding. And I guess that was okay, for a while. But I never stopped hiding, Papa. Never stopped licking my wounds and feeling sorry for myself. The time has come to stop."

"What are you trying to say, Aimee?"

She crossed back to him and knelt in front of his chair. She gathered his hands in hers. "I love you, Papa. I wish I could be everything you want me to be. And I hate to let you down."

She brought his hands to her cheek. "But I have to be everything I want to be first. I have to make sure I don't disappoint myself. I knew that once, but somewhere along the line I forgot it."

"I did not make it easy for you." He shook his head. "I am a hard, demanding man."

"A good man," she corrected. "A good father." She kissed his hands, then released them. "I don't know what I'm going to do, not exactly. And I don't know where I'm going to go. . . I only know I have to make a change. I wanted you to know what was in my heart, Papa."

"I have always known, *chère*." He touched her cheek. "You are a good daughter."

Emotion took her breath. Those words, from him, meant more than any others could. "Thank you, Papa," she whispered.

Aimee stood and crossed back to the window. She wished her answers were there in the dark, in the scent of the jasmine, the flash of the fireflies. But, she knew, the answers she needed could only come from within herself.

"You will take up your camera again?"

"Yes." She smiled. "That much I do know."

"*Bon.*" Roubin nodded. "It is time. You are very talented. I have always been proud of your pictures, of your ability."

Aimee gazed at him, tears of surprise and pleasure pricking her eyes. A moment ago she'd thought he couldn't say anything that would please her more; she'd been wrong. "You never said that before. You never indicated you thought I had talent or—"

"I always thought it." He wheeled across to her. "I was jealous of your camera, *chère*. Jealous of your talent. I knew that one day, it would steal you from me."

Her eyes brimmed, then spilled over.

"Oh, Papa—"

"*Non.*" This time it was he who held up a hand indicating she should listen. "I have done many bad things in my life. Many selfish things. The biggest was trying to make you into the daughter, the person, I wanted you to be. Even when I knew it made you un-happy.''

His eyes grew bright. "For a long time now, I have refused to face your unhappiness.'' He shook his head. "I see, but I do not want to. Because I am a selfish man...because I want you here. With me.''

He sighed heavily. "But you were so happy with Hunter, I could not refuse to see any more.'' He turned his gaze, wet with emotion, on her. "Above all in life, *petite-fille,* I want happiness for you.''

"Oh, Papa...'' She went to him, bent down and hugged him. "I love you so much.''

He hugged her back and for a long time, they just held one another. Finally, Aimee drew away, wiping the tears from her cheeks. "But what are you going to do?''

Roubin brushed at his own cheeks, looking flustered. He cleared his throat. "I have been a fool in so many ways. I have spent the last four years wishing for my old life, growing bitter with my own unhappiness. By wishing for my old life, I have thrown away the life I have now. I am still strong. *Le bon Dieu,* he does not take away my mind. Hunter, he helped me to see these things.

"I will work hard to walk again, Aimee. But, I will be happy with whatever progress *le bon Dieu,* he offers me.'' He squared his shoulders. "I have talked to Cousin Alphonse. He tells me stories. Those boys, calling themselves fishermen. They know nothing!'' Roubin snorted. "They need a man like me to talk to them, to guide them. No one knows the bayou like Roubin Boudreaux!''

Aimee laughed. This was the man she remembered. She hugged him again. "I'm so pleased. So... proud."

Roubin snorted again. "I have been like the *petit-bébé* for too long. Enough!"

"We've come a long way, haven't we, Papa?" she murmured, looking back out the window, to the darkness beyond. Because of Hunter, she acknowledged silently. He'd come into their lives and healed them. If only they'd been able to do the same for him.

"You think of Hunter now, yes?"

Aimee nodded. "Yes."

"You will go after him?"

"No." She drew in a quiet breath. "It's over between us."

"He loves you, *chère*. I know this."

She shook her head, still gazing out at the night. "He wants to, Papa. He does. But he can't. His pain's too great. And I can't settle for less than his whole heart, no matter how much it hurts."

Chapter Twelve

"*Bonjour!*"

Aimee looked up from her portfolio. The woman who had called out the cheery French greeting swept into the store like a whirlwind. Tiny, with fire red hair and startling blue eyes, she looked amazingly like a pixie. Or a leprechaun.

Aimee returned her smile. "Hello."

"And, how are you, *chère?*"

"Fine, thank you," Aimee answered automatically, fighting the urge to tell this stranger the truth—that she had a broken heart, that she was afraid it would never be whole again.

The redheaded pixie clucked her tongue in much the same manner Marie did. Aimee looked at her and experienced the strangest sensation that this woman already *knew* the truth.

Impossible, Aimee told herself, shaking off the sensation. She was oversensitized, her emotions turned upside down and backward because of Hunter. That was all.

Odd, though, Aimee thought, tilting her head, studying the other woman. She didn't recall having met the redhead before, yet something about the way the woman looked at her made her feel she had.

Could she be a friend of Marie's? Aimee wondered. Or of one of the other relatives?

"I'm sorry," Aimee asked, "have we met?"

"Only indirectly." The woman sailed across the room and handed Aimee her business card. "Marla's Small Miracles. Marla, at your service."

"Oh." Aimee stared at the card, the name plucking at her memory.

"*Merci Dieu!* There it is!"

Aimee looked up in time to see Marla scoop up the music box with a flourish. Of course, Aimee remembered. Small Miracles was the shop where Hunter had purchased the box. She drew her eyebrows together. But what was...Marla doing here? How had she found her?

Without taking her eyes from the box, Marla murmured, "Your Hunter, he asked me for directions to this place."

Your Hunter. Aimee squeezed her eyes shut, the words taunting her. Battling back the urge to tell Marla he was no longer *her Hunter,* Aimee folded her arms across her chest. "I see. But what—"

"I had hoped, prayed, the box would still be here." Marla hugged it to her chest. "I must buy it back."

"Pardon me?"

"Maman!" Oliver trotted into the room, dragging his push cart full of blocks behind him. "I hungry. Want..."

He caught sight of Marla, stopped and stared.

"What an adorable child!" Marla exclaimed. The music box still clutched to her breast, Marla bent down and motioned him closer. After sending Aimee a questioning glance, Oliver inched cautiously toward Marla.

He stopped in front of her, and she smiled. "And what is your name, beautiful child?"

"Oliver," he said, studying the woman much the same as Aimee had moments before. Suddenly he smiled, big and brilliantly. "Saw you at hospital. Came to see me."

She laid her hand softly on the top of his head, in the same manner as the priests at Communion. "I am glad you are well, Oliver. But you are mistaken, *petit*. We have not met."

"Yes." He nodded vehemently. "At hospital."

Marla straightened and turned back to Aimee. She smiled and shrugged. "So many people, they look alike."

Aimee bit back a smile. Surely Marla knew that no one looked quite like her. "My son had an ... accident last week. He spent the night in the hospital and...well, it's a miracle he's alive."

"A miracle," Marla repeated, smiling and looking pleased with herself. "That is precisely why I have come. You will sell the box to me?"

Aimee shook her head. "I'm sorry you've come all this way, but the box was a gift from...a friend. It's very precious to me. I couldn't part with it."

Marla clucked her tongue again and set the box back on the counter. "We should not become too attached to material things. After all, is not love the most precious gift of all? The only one worth clinging to?"

Sudden tears stung Aimee's eyes and she blinked against them. If only Hunter had believed her love worth clinging to. If only he had found the gift of her heart the most precious of all.

Aimee cleared her throat. "Of course, that's true. But I—"

"Then, there is nothing to discuss." Marla caught Aimee's hands and looked her directly in the eye. "All the pieces, they are now fitting into place. The plantation this beautiful thing came from, it is to be restored. The owners are desperate to get the box back."

Ashland, Aimee remembered. Hunter had told her about it. She'd been saddened by the plight of the family, saddened by the thought of them having to sell off their heirlooms. But still...

"It is a piece of their history, *chère*. A clue to their past." Marla squeezed her fingers. "It means so very much to them."

"I don't know...." Aimee looked at the box, torn. "As I said, it was a gift—"

"People need box?" Oliver asked suddenly, looking up from his push cart and blocks.

"Yes," Marla murmured, her expression solemn. "Very much."

Oliver tipped his head, studying Marla, puckering his lips in thought. Then he nodded his head. "Give to lady, Maman," he said. "People need."

Aimee gazed at her son. He couldn't have surprised her more if he'd just recited the Declaration of Independence. He loved that music box. He believed Hunter would come back to get it. Why in the world would...he...

Aimee let the thought trail off, and she shifted her gaze back to the pixie-woman. Marla smiled. "I'll pay you one thousand dollars for it."

"A thousand dollars?" Aimee repeated incredulously.

"*Oui*, in cash. Now."

One thousand dollars, Aimee thought. The box would go back to its original owners, where it belonged. She would have enough money to—

"Enough money to set up a darkroom," Marla said, interrupting her thoughts. She gestured to the open portfolio. "These, they are yours?"

"Yes, I..." Aimee drew her eyebrows together, off-balance. The woman seemed to be reading her mind. Ridiculous, of course. But unsettling nonetheless. "Yes, they are."

"They are very good." Marla looked her in the eyes again. "You have a great talent."

"Thank you, but I..." Aimee shook her head. "Thank you."

Marla opened her purse and took out her wallet. She counted out ten one hundred dollar bills and held them out. "This, it is the right thing to do, *chère*. You do not need the box any more."

"Don't need?" Aimee frowned, her thoughts a jumble. "I don't understand. I—"

Marla took Aimee's hands, placed the money in them and curled her fingers around the crisp bills. "Trust me, *chère*. I would not lie to you."

Aimee gazed at the woman. Strangely, she believed her; strangely, she did think it was the right thing to do. Aimee nodded slowly. "All right. It's yours."

Marla smiled. "You will not regret, *non*." She started for the door, the music box nestled in the crook of her arm. She blew Oliver a kiss. "And you, *petit*, you stay away from the bayou."

And then she was gone. Aimee stared after her, feeling as if she'd just gone through the eye of a hurricane. She shifted her gaze from the doorway to the money clutched in her hands. She'd sold her beautiful music box. It, like Hunter, was gone. Now, truly, it was over between them.

Tears pricked at Aimee's eyes, and she blinked against them, not wanting Oliver to see her cry. It was for the best, she told herself, crossing to the screen door and looking out. Every time she'd looked at the music box, she'd been reminded of what she'd almost had. And, now, what she would never have.

Oliver came up beside her. "Kiss make better?"

She shook her head, not trusting herself to speak or meet his eyes.

Reaching up, Oliver curled his fingers around hers. His were sticky. "No cry, Maman. Mr. Hunter come back."

Aimee did look at her son then, her eyes swimming with tears. She tried to smile and failed miserably. "I don't think so, baby."

"Yes." He leaned against her legs and yawned. "Lady told me."

"Lady?"

"One with red hair." He yawned again. "Sleepy, Maman."

Aimee shook her head and lifted him into her arms. He curved his arms around her neck and snuggled his face into the crook of her neck. Her heart turned over. How could she be sad when she still had Oliver? How could she not be deliriously happy when she had so much love?

She thought of Marla and for the first time in days, hope swelled inside her. Everything was going to be okay. She was going to be okay. Kissing the top of her son's head, she said, "I'd better get you some lunch before you fall asleep without it."

The cemetery's ornate wrought-iron gates stood open. For long minutes Hunter waited just beyond, not quite ready to accept their invitation.

A gentle breeze stirred the palm trees and sent the smell of flowers, rich and sweet, wafting through the air. Hunter breathed deeply, but instead of the fragrance of the cemetery's cultivated flowers, the scent of Aimee's night jasmine filled his head, wild, potent and heady.

With the scent came memories that stung his senses just as sharply of the night they'd made love on the porch swing, of the one when they'd sat on the steps and Aimee had poured out her frustrations, and of others when they'd just lain in bed and let the scent drift over them.

Hunter shook his head to rid himself of the memories, sweet though they were, and looked around him. After the Louisiana bayou, California had felt strange. Had looked and smelled strange. Too manicured. Dry and earth-toned instead of humid and vividly green. Hunter slipped his hands into his trouser pockets, moving his gaze over the vast cemetery, its green a brilliant contrast to the sepia and gold of the mountains.

He'd come to say goodbye to his past. And hello to the future. He could not have one without letting go of the other; they were inextricably bound.

Aimee.

God, he'd missed her. Her smile. Her husky laugh. The way she looked at him, as if he were the only man in the world who mattered, the way she melted in his arms. But most of all, he'd missed the way she made him feel.

Alive.

It had taken leaving her to see how much he needed her. How much he loved her.

And how much he loved Oliver. His son.

Hunter looked down at the teddy bear he had clutched in his hands, matted and worn from hours of loving abuse. Pete's love. He rubbed his fingers over the bear's fuzzy head. All their personal belongings had been taken by the fire. All that had remained were the few pictures he'd had in his office, his wallet. This bear he'd found under the front seat of Ginny's car.

He hadn't discovered it until weeks after the funeral, weeks after he'd buried Pete with a new toy. He'd always felt bad about that.

Hunter brought the toy to his face, to his nose, and breathed deeply. It smelled of Pete still. Or maybe, Hunter acknowledged, that was only his imagination.

He rubbed the bear lightly against his cheek. Pete had known and loved this toy. He'd slept with it crushed against his face, had hugged it, had dragged it around behind him. It hadn't been his favorite, but it should have been buried with him. Pete shouldn't have had to be buried with a stranger.

The future, Hunter thought again, walking through the gates. He followed the winding walkways, lined with flowering bushes, knowing the way by heart even though he'd made this trip only once. On the day his family had been buried. It had hurt too much for him to come again. Until today.

Hunter reached the plots, the marble markers he'd picked out while still in shock. He stared at the side-by-side graves, his heart beating slowly and heavily against the wall of his chest.

Mother and child. His wife, his son. It hurt. It would forever. Their deaths had been a senseless waste of life. He'd loved them with all of his heart. Just as passionately, he hated that they'd died. The way they'd died.

But the pain inside him had changed. The anger had shifted, his feelings of blame and guilt with it. He'd changed.

Hunter shook his head. For five years he'd wished he were here with Ginny and Pete, had wished he'd died, too. He didn't any more. He wanted to live.

Hunter closed his eyes and his head filled with images from the past, filled with happy memories of times he and Ginny and Pete had spent together: the moment of Pete's birth, when he and Ginny had looked at one another with wonder and love; the night he'd asked Ginny to marry him; Pete's first step; their wedding; Pete's first birthday.

They were memories of life. Of living. Of loving. They filled him with happiness and light. They chased away the nightmares, the endless cold.

Aimee had given this back to him. The ability to remember. The ability to feel. To love. Aimee had given him back life.

Hunter squatted down in front of Pete's resting place. He'd arranged for fresh flowers to be placed weekly on the graves, and the ones that adorned the plots now were bright and cheering.

Hunter brushed wilted petals and leaves lovingly away. Emotion welled in his chest until he thought he would burst from it. But it didn't frighten him as it would have only a week ago, and he didn't try to fight it off or control it. Grieving, letting go, was a part of life, awful though it was.

"Hey, Buddy," he murmured thickly. "Brought you something. An old friend." Hunter propped the teddy bear carefully against the headstone, then arranged the flowers around it. "Thought you might want the little guy around. Remember the time you took it in the bathtub with you?" He shook his head. "You couldn't understand why he couldn't swim."

Hunter smiled at that memory and a dozen others that rushed into his head with it. "I miss you, Buddy. So much." Hunter thought of Roubin and of faith. "But... it's okay now. I know that wherever you are, wherever heaven is, you're being loved."

Hunter drew in a ragged breath, his chest heavy and aching. "You have a brother now." Hunter thought of

Oliver and smiled. "You'd like him, I know you would. And I know you would have been a good big brother."

Hunter reached out and touched Pete's marker, moving his fingers slowly across the chiseled letters. "He can be shy, Pete. Too cautious." Hunter thought of the bayou and a shudder moved over him. "Sometimes not cautious enough. If you were around, you'd show him the ropes.

"I'll tell him about you," he continued, his voice husky with tears. "You'll always be my baby, Pete. And . . . I'll . . . always love you."

Hunter shifted his gaze from Pete's grave to Ginny's. How did one do this? he wondered. How did he tell the memory of the woman he'd once loved about the woman he loved now? And strange, he acknowledged, how it felt at once awkward and right.

As he had with Pete's, Hunter straightened up the grave site, brushing away dead flowers and leaves, rearranging the live ones. "Ah, Gin," he said finally, softly, "there's so much I have to say to you, so many things I didn't get to say to you. Like goodbye." His throat closed and he worked to clear it. "I couldn't come before this. Because I blamed myself. For the fire. For your and Pete's deaths. Because of those damn locks, because I wasn't home to protect you."

He shook his head, thinking of the wasted years, the debilitating guilt. "Accidents happen, Ginny. I realize that now. Tragedies occur. They're a part of living. I'm not to blame. No one is."

He reached out and touched her marker, the smooth marble warm beneath his fingers. "I couldn't face my own guilt. I couldn't face the pain of living knowing that you and Pete had died. For five years I ceased living to avoid the pain.

"You wouldn't have liked the man I'd become. Cold and controlled, so wrapped up in my own misery I couldn't even see love when I had it in my hands."

In the distance Hunter heard the sound of laughter. Children's laughter. It rippled over his senses like music, and he smiled. "I want to live, Ginny. Aimee made me see that. She brought me back to the world of the living. She's a remarkable woman. Strong and beautiful and full of life. You'd like her."

Hunter lifted his face to the cloudless blue sky, drinking in the beauty of the day. "I never thought I'd feel anything again, and now . . . I love her so much it's like a miracle."

The sound of the children came closer. They appeared from around a corner, a boy and girl, their arms filled with flowers. As they saw him, their mother tried to hush them.

"I'm sorry," the woman said as they passed, her cheeks crimson with embarrassment.

Hunter smiled. "Don't be. They're children, they're supposed to laugh. Besides, we like it. We like it a lot."

The trio moved on, and Hunter reached out and touched Ginny's marker one last time. He smoothed his fingers over the sun-warmed marble, then dropped his hand. "Goodbye, Ginny. Take good care of our baby up there. I love you."

Even as he murmured the words, he thought of Aimee. And of the life they would have together. Whispering a final goodbye, Hunter stood and turned away from the past and headed toward his future.

* * *

Aimee stood on the gallery and gazed at the horizon and at the most spectacular sunset she'd ever seen. Brilliant pinks and lavenders, fiery reds and oranges, a hint of gold, they transformed the sky into an artist's canvas. Sighing, she rested her head against one of the cypress columns. How could nature be capable of such an incredible feat when she couldn't even put Hunter out of her mind?

She had tried. She'd immersed herself in her plans for the future—attempting to decide where she and Oliver were going to live, contacting art galleries about handling her photographs, pricing darkroom equipment. But even filling every minute of the day with activity, she'd still missed Hunter. Still ached for him.

Still wished things had turned out differently.

At the sound of tires turning on to the shell drive, Aimee shifted her attention away from the sunset and her own brooding thoughts. She watched the car as it inched down the long drive in her direction. Who would be calling at this hour? she wondered, not recognizing the car. And on a Sunday, no less?

Hunter.

A trembling started in the pit of her stomach, and Aimee sternly told herself to put that thought out of her mind. A beautiful sky did not a miracle make. Hunter had been gone ten days. He wasn't coming back, no matter what she wished, no matter what she felt in her heart.

No matter how often Oliver assured her he was.

The car stopped. The driver-side door swung open; her breath caught on a prayer.

Hunter stepped out.

Heart thundering, Aimee gripped the column for support. He'd come back. He'd come after her.

She didn't move, she couldn't. She was afraid to breathe. Inside her hope warred with the numbing fear that he'd come back for the music box, or Oliver, or anything else besides her.

He started toward her, his blue gaze unwaveringly on hers. He hesitated only once, at the bottom of the gallery stairs. He tipped his face up to hers. Behind him the sky blazed with color.

For long, breathless moments, they stared silently at one another.

Hunter broke the silence first. "No hello for an old friend, Aimee?"

She shook her head, fear a living thing inside her. "Not until you tell me why you've come. I couldn't bear to say hello only to say goodbye again."

He climbed the stairs, stopping before her. He reached out and cupped her cheeks. "No goodbyes, never again."

The breath shuddered past her lips, hope ballooned inside her. "I told you not to come back unless—"

"I love you, Aimee. All the way and with everything I am and have. You brought me back to life, you showed me how to feel again. How to love."

She brought her hands to his chest, searching his gaze for a clue to his sudden change of heart. "I want to believe you," she whispered. "I want to believe so badly I ache with it. But . . . I'm afraid to believe too much. I'm afraid to hope for too much. I don't want to be hurt again."

He threaded his fingers through her hair. "You worked your magic on me long ago, Aimee Boudreaux. But I was too blind, too afraid, to see the truth. I came to La Fin because I couldn't forget you. I told myself to keep emotionally distant from you, to stay removed from your life. You drew me in. To your life. Your warmth. I began to feel and the cold, with its nightmares, began to recede.

"I called what was happening to me, what I was feeling, other things." He laughed softly, still incredulous over his own inability to see the truth. "I made excuses. Rationalized about how I had nothing to give, about how you were better off without me."

Aimee searched his gaze. "But... why?"

"Because I loved you already," he said simply. "And I was terrified. Before I left, your father accused me of being just that, of leaving you because of that fear. Your father's a smart man. I lost my family once, I didn't think I could stand the pain of losing another."

"So," she murmured, "you didn't allow yourself to be loved. Didn't allow anyone get close to you."

"Self-preservation."

She stroked his cheek. "But so lonely."

"When we found Oliver... all my fears became a reality. It was the most awful moment. It brought all the horror back." Hunter drew in a ragged breath. "I thought I was going to have to bury another son. I shut down, then I bolted."

The image of Oliver in the water, of those minutes when she'd thought they'd lost him, filled her head again, and she shuddered. She could only imagine what it must have been like for Hunter having already lost Pete. "What happened?" she asked, her eyes swimming with tears. "What made you—"

"Realize how much I love you?" Aimee smiled, and he touched one corner of her mouth with a fingertip. "The pain of living without you was unbearable. And so senseless. Out of fear of losing you, I was throwing you away. Just as I had been throwing life away."

"Never again," she whispered. "I'll never waste one precious moment of the life we've been given."

Hunter tumbled her against his chest and caught her mouth in a searing kiss. For one long moment Aimee allowed herself the pleasure of his arms, his kiss. Then she eased herself free of them.

She wanted to simply melt against him. She wanted to take what he offered and not worry about the past. But she couldn't. Not yet. "You haven't mentioned Ginny or Pete. And I have to know, Hunter. I have to ask. What about them? I can't compete with ghosts. And I won't."

Aimee clasped her hands in front of her, waiting, bracing herself for his answer. She understood now what she needed to be happy; if Hunter couldn't say the words she needed him to, she would have to tell him goodbye.

"I love Ginny," he said after a moment. "You don't stop loving someone because they're dead. But it's a memory of love, a love of the past. One that doesn't interfere with or dim the present." He lowered his voice to a husky murmur. "Or the future."

He brought her back against his chest, breathing in the sweet, spicy scent of her. "And I love Oliver," he continued. "The way a father must. I want us to be together, to be a family." He buried his hands in her hair. "I've put my ghosts behind me, Aimee. I'm a free man with everything to give."

She relaxed then, curling her arms around him, holding on to him in a way she'd been afraid to before. This time, she knew, he would be there for her. Forever and always. "I love you so much. I thought it was over. I thought—"

"I know." He stroked her hair. "I'm sorry I hurt you."

She tilted her head back and met his eyes. "That doesn't matter, not any more. As long as you love me."

"I do." He brushed his mouth against hers, lightly, savoring. "I can't promise that there won't be nightmares. I wish I could, but—"

She placed a finger gently against his lips, quieting him. "They're part of life, of being human. And as long as you love me, the nightmares can't touch us."

"Then they never will again," he murmured, catching her hands and lacing their fingers. "I can't believe I almost let you slip away."

Hands still joined, he lowered his mouth to hers. No kiss had ever been so satisfying. So complete. Finally, after all the time that had passed, all the hurt, they would be together. Without ghosts of the past to cloud their future.

After several moments, Hunter broke the contact, breathing hard. He rested his forehead against hers. "Damn, I missed you. I was a crazy man. I couldn't eat or sleep. My temper—"

"Mine, too. I thought you weren't coming back." She laughed. "But Oliver never lost faith in you."

"Really?" he said, pleased. "I was afraid he'd never forgive me."

"He was hurt at first. Terribly. But he kept saying an angel told him you'd be back."

"An angel?" Hunter shook his head, grinning. "Pass that one by me again."

Aimee rubbed her cheek against his chest. "Mmm ... a red-headed angel who visited him in the hospital. He thinks it was Marla. You know, from Small Miracles."

Hunter drew his eyebrows together. "Now, I really am confused. When did he meet Marla?"

Aimee hesitated, then quickly explained what had happened, how Marla had shown up and convinced her to sell the box. "It was strange, I kept feeling she could read my mind." Aimee laughed lightly. "And Oliver was certain she'd visited him in the hospital. He's still talking about it."

"It's not uncommon," Hunter said. "He'd had a shock, a brush with death. People report all sorts of things after an experience like that."

"That's what I thought, too."

Hunter smiled. "As for Marla, I'm not so sure she isn't a brick or two short of a full load. There's just something ... different about her."

"Mmm." Aimee curved her arms around his waist. "I liked her, though. Something about her made me feel good. Hopeful."

She met his eyes then, searching. "About the music box, I hope you're not hurt or—"

"I'm not." He planted another kiss on her mouth. "Marla may be strange, but she was right. Love is the most precious gift of all. And right now, I'd like us to go share it with somebody else.''

Aimee held out her hand. "Let's."

Joining hands, they went in search of their son.

Epilogue

"I think we should, Hunter." Aimee threaded through the French Quarter crowds, on her way to Royal Street. "After all, even you said she was responsible for getting us together."

"*Partly* responsible," Hunter said, catching up with Aimee. Oliver sat on his shoulders, and he shifted the boy's weight to a more comfortable position. "Besides, couldn't we just send the woman an invitation?"

"Sure." Aimee laughed. "But we're here now. Let's just stop."

"No stop," Oliver announced. "Like horsey ride. Keep going."

"I'm with you, Tiger. But your *maman,* when she gets an idea in her head ..." He clucked his tongue in an imitation of Marie. "Just ask your *pépère*. He'll tell you how stubborn she is."

Aimee laughed again and looked at the business card in her hand, then checked for an address. "Small Miracles should be just up ahead."

They walked in silence for the moments it took to reach the shop. Aimee stopped in front of the address, her spirits sinking. She gazed at the deserted storefront, then checked the number again. "Is this the place, Hunter? Could the address on the card be wrong?"

Hunter glanced around. "No, this is it. I remember the shop next door."

"Lady gone," Oliver said sadly. "No more angel."

Aimee peered in the shop's window. The interior was empty save for a few dusty-looking fixtures. "It was only a week ago that she showed up in La Fin," Aimee murmured. "How could she be gone now?"

"You folks looking for Marla?"

Aimee turned. The shopkeeper from the next store over stood in her doorway, lighting a cigarette. "Yes." Aimee smiled, encouraged. "Do you know where she went?"

"Boston, I think." The woman shook her head and blew out a long stream of smoke. "I've been in business here on Royal Street thirty-five years. But Marla, she just up and left after a matter of only months. Her business looked brisk, too." The woman shrugged. "But who knows?"

Aimee sighed. "Thank you for your help anyway."

"Say..." The shopkeeper narrowed her eyes. "She left something, said I would know who it was for when they called." The woman shook her head. "She was always doing stuff like that. Strange. Hold on, I'll get it."

Aimee looked at Hunter. He lifted his shoulders. A moment later the woman hurried back out, a small, cream-colored envelope in her hand. She held it out for Aimee, even as she smiled at a couple of tourists as they headed inside her shop.

"Here you go," she said hurriedly, obviously anxious to get back inside her store. "I hope you're the ones. If not..." She shrugged as if to say "keep it anyway" and ducked back into her shop.

Aimee watched her go, then carefully ripped open the envelope and pulled out the card. Engraved in gold, it read:

Love, the greatest miracle of all.

Aimee caught her breath and handed the card to Hunter.

He read it and met her eyes, the expression in his incredibly soft. "She's right," he murmured, his voice choked with emotion. "I know that now." He held out his hand. "I love you, Aimee Boudreaux."

Aimee caught his hand, curling her fingers around his, tears of joy stinging her eyes. "And I love you, Hunter Powell."

Turning, they started for the future. Together.

*   *   *   *   *

Look for Magnolia Dawn *in December 93...*
Only from Silhouette Special Edition.

It takes a very special man to win *That* **SPECIAL** *Woman!*

She's friend, wife, mother—she's you! And beside each Special Woman stands a wonderfully special man. It's a celebration of our heroines—and the men who become part of their lives.

Look for these exciting titles from Silhouette Special Edition:

August MORE THAN HE BARGAINED FOR by Carole Halston
Heroine: Avery Payton—a woman struggling for independence falls for the man next door.

September A HUSBAND TO REMEMBER by Lisa Jackson
Heroine: Nikki Carrothers—a woman without memories meets the man she should never have forgotten...her husband.

October ON HER OWN by Pat Warren
Heroine: Sara Shepard—a woman returns to her hometown and confronts the hero of her childhood dreams.

November GRAND PRIZE WINNER! by Tracy Sinclair
Heroine: Kelley McCormick—a woman takes the trip of a lifetime and wins the greatest prize of all...love!

December POINT OF DEPARTURE by Lindsay McKenna
(Women of Glory)
Heroine: Lt. Callie Donovan—a woman takes on the system and must accept the help of a kind and sexy stranger.

Don't miss THAT SPECIAL WOMAN! each month—from some of your special authors! Only from Silhouette Special Edition!

TAKE A WALK ON THE
DARK SIDE OF LOVE WITH

October is the shivery season, when chill winds blow and
shadows walk the night. Come along with us into a haunting
world where love and danger go hand in hand, where
passions will thrill you and dangers will chill you. Silhouette's
second annual collection from the dark side of love brings
you three perfectly haunting tales from three of our most
bewitching authors:

Kathleen Korbel
Carla Cassidy
Lori Herter

Haunting a store near you this October.

Only from 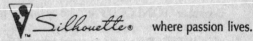 where passion lives.

Silhouette®

SPECIAL EDITION®

WILD RIVER TRILOGY

by Laurie Paige

Come meet the wild McPherson men and see how these three sexy bachelors are tamed!

In HOME FOR A WILD HEART (SE #828) you got to know Kerrigan McPherson. Now meet the rest of the family:

A PLACE FOR EAGLES, September 1993—
Keegan McPherson gets the surprise of his life.

THE WAY OF A MAN, November 1993—
Paul McPherson finally meets his match.

Don't miss any of these exciting titles—only for our readers and only from Silhouette Special Edition!

Silhouette Books has done it again!

Opening night in October has never been as exciting! Come watch as the curtain rises and romance flourishes when the stars of tomorrow make their debuts today!

Revel in Jodi O'Donnell's STILL SWEET ON HIM—
Silhouette Romance #969
...as Callie Farrell's renovation of the family homestead leads her straight into the arms of teenage crush Drew Barnett!

Tingle with Carol Devine's BEAUTY AND THE BEASTMASTER—
Silhouette Desire #816
...as legal eagle Amanda Tarkington is carried off by wrestler Bram Masterson!

Thrill to Elyn Day's A BED OF ROSES—
Silhouette Special Edition #846
...as Dana Whitaker's body and soul are healed by sexy physical therapist Michael Gordon!

Believe when Kylie Brant's McLAIN'S LAW —
Silhouette Intimate Moments #528
...takes you into detective Connor McLain's life as he falls for psychic—and suspect—Michele Easton!

Catch the classics of tomorrow—*premiering* today—
only from ✶ *Silhouette*

MEN MADE IN AMERICA

Fifty red-blooded, white-hot, true-blue hunks from every
State in the Union!

Beginning in May, look for MEN MADE IN AMERICA!
Written by some of our most popular authors, these
stories feature fifty of the strongest, sexiest men, each
from a different state in the union!

Two titles available every other month at your favorite
retail outlet.

In September, look for:

DECEPTIONS by Annette Broadrick (California)
STORMWALKER by Dallas Schulze (Colorado)

In November, look for:

STRAIGHT FROM THE HEART by Barbara Delinsky
(Connecticut)
AUTHOR'S CHOICE by Elizabeth August (Delaware)

You won't be able to resist MEN MADE IN AMERICA!